MUD SEASON

MUD SEASON

SHORT FICTION

BY KRISTINA BAER

PARK PLACE PUBLICATIONS
PACIFIC GROVE, CA

PARK PLACE PUBLICATIONS
Pacific Grove, California

For George
"Ni vus sanz mei, ne jeo sanz vus."
Neither you without me, nor I without you.
Chievrefoil, Marie de France (Lais, 1160-1170)

CONTENTS

Mud Season ◊ 1

Past Imperfect ◊ 25

Hermit Crabs ◊ 43

Fairy Lights ◊ 59

Fireflies ◊ 87

Sheba ◊ 103

Acknowledgments

Mud Season

On Saturday morning, the weekend after my retirement ceremony, I got up at 7, had coffee with Lydia, and left for my office. I planned to spend the morning clearing drawers and file cabinets. I'd finished sorting my books—the dictionaries and reference books, I would donate; all the official university materials I would leave for my successor. The rest, my personal library, I would take with me when Lydia and I moved to North Bennington.

At the foot of the driveway, I glanced back at Lydia, standing in the doorway with Blue, our Labrador, sitting beside her. I waved. She waved. This had been our weekday routine every day for thirty-five years.

Driving to the University, my coffee mug in the console holder beside me, I looked straight ahead. Traffic permitting, I could time the drive to make the green light at the main intersection—going and coming. Once or twice, I'd been held up as much as five minutes. Colleagues who lived in the outskirts of Burlington complained about traffic delays lasting a half-hour or more. I did my best to sympathize. Privately, I gloated: I could complete my 12-block commute in under 10 minutes most days. Today, my last, was no exception.

In the parking lot, I ignored the sign warning me to park in my assigned spot or be fined. The lot was empty. If I got a ticket, it would be the first. And the last. One step at a time, I told myself. In my head, it was my father's voice I heard. He had an aphorism for every occasion.

I found a message taped to the door of my office: "Randall: EVERY day is the first day of the rest of your life. Don't waste a minute. Tom." Tom, a former student, now an assistant professor and colleague in the English Department, shared my passion for crime fiction, and my dad's aphorism habit.

I set my mug and keys on the desk and put the boxes on the floor. I'd bought two packs of six each, figuring if I needed more, I could go down to the university store to buy them. I looked out the window. The quad was deserted. In a week, when summer school began, students would once again cross back and forth to class, pausing to chat or sit on the lawn, eating lunch, drinking coffee, some taking a break to toss a Frisbee.

Most days, I'd spent much of my time here, grading papers, writing lectures, occasionally looking out the window at the view of the quadrangle, which changed with the seasons, a predictable variation year to year. Twenty-five years ago, asphalt paving had replaced the brick walkways that crisscrossed the lawn. I still missed the contrast between the weathered brick and the green grass in the spring and summer, the students lounging on the grass, or hunched against the wind and snow as they hurried to class. How many had passed by over the years, unaware that I was up here, doing what professors do—preparing my classes, grading papers, glancing down at them from time to time?

The campus clock chimed. 8 o' clock. Better get started if I wanted to finish by lunchtime.

"Live every day as if it were your last." Dad again. I certainly hope I'm not sorting and boxing books and old lectures on my last day, I tell him. In his view, compressed into aphorisms, much of life was predictable, if not bearable. Now 65 (Dad died at 70) I nod, smile, and move on without stating the obvious: Life is full of surprises. Not quite an aphorism, but as a truism, it will do.

◦ ◦ ◦

I unlocked and opened the top drawer of the file cabinet to the left of my desk. As I removed the first half-dozen folders—typed lectures organized by course—it hit me: I wasn't just moving the folders from one place to another, where they would be close at hand to review at the beginning of the next semester. There would be no next semester. I planned to box and take the folders to our lawyer, who had agreed to shred them. I heard myself as if giving a lecture about this process, explaining it as a kind of burial. Not that much of a stretch, really. Suddenly, I saw myself standing at the lectern, facing a lecture hall filled with freshmen, heard myself begin my lecture on "Hamlet":

"What's wrong with Hamlet? From the start, Shakespeare's challenge is to convince us that "What's wrong with Hamlet?" is the wrong question. The right question, the important question is: "What's wrong with Denmark?"

One year after I gave this lecture, a student, a young woman, came to me in tears. "Those awful people! Poor Hamlet!" Yes, I told her. Romeo and Juliet, and Hamlet, are destroyed by their pitiless corrupt families, whose feckless schemes undermine all that is good and decent in the world.

I would never again give these lectures—or any others, for that matter—to anyone, eager freshmen or jaded seniors. I would never again experience the thrill of watching one or two students smile and nod, never again comfort a student whose eyes had been opened to the horrors we humans inflict upon one another. And, of course, I'd never have to grade another paper written by an indifferent student whose mind was elsewhere.

How many hours had I devoted to reading, outlining, and writing, then editing my lectures? By now, I imagined the time would add up to several years, because I revised and updated my lectures regularly, a point of pride: In my department, I was the only one who did.

Early on, I used to spend several hours seven days a week in the library or in my office organizing my thoughts, writing and rewriting lecture drafts until I had what I thought sufficient to enlighten my students, if not entertain them. I made sure to speak to them, not at them, to help them understand what they were reading and why.

In time, I became the department's go-to guy for the courses required of freshmen and English majors. I enjoyed giving these lectures because I knew, as my students did not, that most of them would never again read or write about Great Works by Great Authors. Here, in my lecture hall and in my classroom, they had a once-in-a-lifetime opportunity, one they just might remember years from now, perhaps when they, like me, were packing up elements of their former life in preparation for a new one. Some of them might tell their own children about Hamlet, or David Copperfield, or Emma, about how they learned to look at their own lives differently, thanks to a character in a book.

My colleagues respected my work in the classroom. Few of them had the patience to do the research and the winnowing required to do what I did, to teach students who might not major in English Lit, or those who would become majors, who lacked a foundation. On the other hand, I hadn't the ambition to pursue the literary theories, fads that came and went.

I did my job to ensure my students—our students—learned something new about something old, that they had a glimpse of traditions older than they, that likely would outlive them. That, it seemed to me, was what they were there for. They'd never heard of Chaucer? Well, then, let's tell them Chaucer's story. Let's stage readings of "Canterbury Tales." Who was Virginia Woolf and why was she important? Let's read "A Room of One's Own," and, while we're at it, let's talk about some of the reasons there aren't more published women writers—in all languages, including English. I wanted my students to remember what they learned, not the name of the person who taught the course. That way, what they learned in my classes would be folded into their own life history. That's what I hoped they would take with them.

◊ ◊ ◊

By the time I finished emptying the file cabinets and sorting the books, I had filled and taped all 12 boxes, which I carried one by one down to the car. I placed my office keys on the empty desktop beside the lamp and stood there for a moment in the middle of the room, now awaiting the next occupant, and looked out onto the quad. Eyes shut, I imagined standing at the edge of Lake Paran in North Bennington on a breezy afternoon, watching the cloud reflections, listening to the water lapping at the beach. The "what now?" feeling I'd had over the last few weeks began to lift. Yes, I was looking forward to what came next.

As I closed the door the nameplate hanging on the wall to the left caught my eye. "Professor Randall Johnson, English Department." I used the screwdriver I'd brought just in case to remove it. "No dangling modifiers!" My laugh echoed faintly through the empty corridor.

That's when it hit me: I would never pass this way again. Today was the last time I would have coffee with Lydia, drive to the campus, park in my usual place, greet the same people I greeted daily, climb the 40 stairs to my office, unlock the door, and begin my day. I would never again face twenty sleep-deprived (or hung-over) undergraduates, whose interest in what I had to tell them waxed and waned as the term wore on.

I'd plowed my last furrow. I was headed out to pasture.

◊ ◊ ◊

In the parking lot, as I loaded the last box into the car, someone called my name. I turned around.

Jared, my jogging partner, crossed the parking lot. "Books?"

"Bumf," I told him. "Years of lectures, class notes, seminar outlines…"

He grinned. "Too bad you can't sell the lectures to the person who replaces you." He eyed the boxes. "And the books?"

"I boxed the ones I'm keeping. I'll donate the rest to the library."

"Does North Bennington even have a library?"

"Sure does. The John G. McCullough Free Library."

Jared raised his eyebrows.

"It's not like we're moving to the boondocks, Jared."

He laughed. He knew I was relieved to leave the university—and Burlington—for the place that had been my second home for years.

o o o

At the end of every year after I started teaching at UVM, Lydia and I closed our house in Burlington and spent the summer in the house I'd inherited from my grandparents in North Bennington. Evenings, we walked down to Main Street, past Powers Market and the library on our way to Lake Paran, where I'd learned to swim and where I'd spent two summers as a lifeguard. After I passed my orals at Harvard, I proposed to Lydia on the beach there under a full moon.

Even now, I sometimes fall asleep lulled by memories of floating under a brilliant summer sky, listening to the shouts of kids playing volleyball on the beach, breathing in the scent of apples ripening in the orchard on the far shore. Most of these memories include a dog, one of a long line of retrievers, barking excitedly, waiting for me to toss a ball, lunging into the water well before the ball splashes down. Labradors and golden retrievers, they retrieved for the sheer joy of bringing the ball back, eager for the next toss.

Lydia and I, both native Vermonters, prefer the size and pace of the villages where we grew up. Our daughters, Laura and Ellen, call North Bennington our "lean and mean" retirement community—no heated swimming pool, no pool table, no tennis court, no weekly bridge parties, no meal plan. They roll their eyes when I remind them about the lake.

"Isn't it ice-covered until July?" Ellen teases.

"There's no movie theater, Dad," Laura chimes in.

"We'll survive. We're not city folks, you know." I've said this often enough, but it bears repeating, now, especially, as we are packing to go. One hundred and twenty miles south of Burlington, North Bennington is its opposite in size and ambition: With its single block of shops and Powers Market, Main Street looks much as it did a hundred years ago. That's fine with us.

o o o

A day or two after we arrived, as soon as Lydia and I finished unpacking we both let go, little by little, settling into the house. Lydia set up her watercolors and books in what had been my grandmother's sewing room. I shelved my books in my grandfather's study. Blue had his den under the staircase in the front hall, where he could keep one eye on us and the house, the other on the front door. Like most of the Labs in my life, as a puppy he had learned to swim in Lake Paran. Like me, he could have made his way to the lake, eyes closed. Lydia and I both knew he wouldn't be with us much longer. We were happy for him to have this time with us in his favorite place.

o o o

I grew up with dogs, retrievers mostly. I still have a photo from when I'm six months old, curled up beside our black Lab, Clementine, who gazes into the camera, alert and vigilant. She died when I was seven. For weeks, I slept in her kennel, burrowed into the Army blanket my dad had saved from his tour in Korea. I knew its worn patches and holes as well as I knew the cowlicks on Clementine's elbows and the soft spot under her chin.

Weeks later, my mother washed the blanket. That night I pulled it over my head, cupping it tight against my nose, sniffing for Clementine's warm scent. Nothing remained. I turned on my light and searched it inch by inch until I found a single black dog hair wedged into the tightly woven binding. In my dream Clementine stretched out beside me, her head next to mine, her breath fluttering in my ear.

Long after the arrival of our next dog, a golden retriever I named Abby, I slept with Clementine's blanket rolled up alongside me in my bunkbed next to the wall, where Clementine had often slept. When I left for college, I packed the blanket into the trunk where I kept odds and ends—a model sailboat I built from a kit; the shells I collected on the beach in Wellfleet; my k-12 report cards, and a few Scout badges. There was plenty of room for the blanket, by then so tattered and frayed you'd never have guessed it had kept my father warm through the last spring in Korea.

Clementine taught me how dogs love and how to love them back. Her scent, the texture of her fur, the sound of her breathing, like the bass note of a complex musical chord, were the foundation. The dogs who came later throughout my life built up and out from there, adding sharps, flats, trills, and grace notes.

Once Lydia got to know Annie, the Lab I had when we met, you'd never have guessed Annie was her first dog. Lydia was a natural. Without being told how, she sensed how to make eye contact and how to recognize the moment the puppies we trained together began to observe and attend to us.

"They're so much better at this than we are, Randall." She laughed. "If only humans could learn to watch one another the way dogs watch and learn from us."

o o o

Blue died in his sleep at the end of our first year in North Bennington. Except for his rambunctious first year, he had always sought to please us, to accommodate our needs. He was a no-muss-no-fuss dog until the end.

"Do you remember the time Blue brought home the kitten?" I asked Lydia one morning, a couple of months later.

"That was Sally, not Blue," she reminded me.

"Of course, it was," I laughed, surprised that I'd forgotten. Sally, our second Lab, had tried and failed to have puppies, but her hormones kept reminding her of her pregnancy for weeks after she'd been spayed. We didn't realize she had the kitten in her mouth until she dropped it in my lap. Our vet named her "Kitty," fed her with an eye dropper, and took her home, where she grew up to be a ferocious mouser.

Lydia eyed my belt, a notch looser than usual, and patted my belly. "Time to get another dog to walk, Randall." Every weekday afternoon when I came home, I had walked Blue. He had learned my schedule and waited for me just inside the door, lying under the hook where we'd hung his leash. When he got sick, before we knew why, Lydia figured if we just found the right combination of pills, he'd get his energy back. "You'll be walking him again in no time," Lydia had assured me. She researched and discussed every possible remedy with me and with our vet, hopeful to the end.

o o o

Of course, we talked about getting another dog. "I know you. You'll enjoy having a puppy around," Lydia said. We'd had Labs and a Lab-mix, all trained—and loved—from the moment they came to us. I liked training them. So did Lydia. She discerned early what made each of them unique, their individual tics and talents.

Sophie, for example, was a thief from the time she came to us at three months old until she died at twelve. The things she took—a spool of thread, a shoelace, and socks, of course—all ended up in her bed, buried under her blanket. Once she'd found and hidden them, she lost interest. For a few days, she'd sigh in her sleep, as if mourning her lost treasures. Then, the game would begin again, abetted by the girls and Lydia, who kept a basket of odds and ends for her. She'd hide two or three of them around the house.

Sophie did the rest. Her talent gave her a head start. She became a phenomenal tracker encouraged by Laura and Ellen, who played hide and seek with her. The vet once asked if we'd consider giving her up to an organization that trained dogs like Sophie for rescue work.

Then there was Justa. He was a Lab-mix, our only rescue dog, "Justadog," we called him. He refused to settle at night without one of my slippers in his bed. He slept curled up with it under his chin. Eventually, when that slipper fell apart, we got him another. At first, he wouldn't accept the substitute, searching for the original, indoors and out. Lydia suggested I wear the slipper for a week or two. That did the trick. From then on, it was Justa's slipper.

I often wondered how he'd gotten lost or abandoned—we never knew for sure. Although he was happy with us, I knew the slipper represented a loss he'd never get over.

○ ○ ○

In March, six months after Blue died, I came home from running errands in Bennington. A woman I didn't recognize sat in the living room with Lydia. In her late-twenties, I guessed, she was dressed in slacks and a fisherman's sweater, her long, curly blonde hair held in check by a narrow headband. She'd left her boots by the door and was wearing a pair of Lydia's slippers.

"Randall, this is Suzanne," Lydia said, smiling at us both. "Suzanne raises standard poodles in Shaftsbury. She has one four-month-old puppy left. A female. I'd like you to meet her, see what you think. About the puppy." She winked at me. "I told Suzanne she's my birthday present."

"Darn! I was hoping to surprise you."

We all laughed. Lydia's eyes gleamed.

After Lydia and I put away the groceries, we sat at the kitchen table with our tea. "Just one question."

Lydia grinned and nodded. "I know what's coming."

"A standard poodle? Really?"

She held up one finger. "They don't shed." A second finger. "They're problem-solvers, which means they practically train themselves." Third finger. "Often, they're 'sensitive-intuitive' types." She looked at me. "Of course, you're skeptical. Trust me, Randall. This is a good idea."

o o o

The next morning, I drove to Shaftsbury. Since Lydia had already met the puppy, she had suggested I go by myself. "I really do want you to make up your own mind, Randall," she'd told me. "Yes, she'll be my birthday present, but you'll have to live with her, too, so let's be sure about her."

It was a bright day, in the low 40s. The snow was melting, the beginning of mud season. At least for her first few weeks with us, this puppy wouldn't be racing around loose in the mud. Maybe the gloppy conditions would calm her down enough that leash training would proceed smoothly and quickly. I could hear Lydia's scoff: "Since when has any puppy we've ever brought home behaved calmly about anything—except sleep."

Suzanne lived in an old farmhouse set back from the road—plain and simple, like the two sugar maples that stood at the end of the driveway. I parked behind the house, near a small barn. It looked freshly painted, red with white trim, and its roof had new green shingles. Bleating sheep sheltered in a fenced area beside it.

A plume of smoke drifted up from the house's central chimney. The woodpile, neatly stacked with lengths to fit a woodstove, stood outside the back door beside the porch. A red-and-black checked hunting jacket hung from a peg next to the back door. Excited woofs greeted me as I climbed the back steps.

Inside, in the kitchen, the puppy and her mother, Bella, pranced around and circled one another on the faded linoleum, pushing each other and us. Their cream-colored coats thick and curly, they ran back and forth between Suzanne and me as if making a difficult choice: Suzanne, because she was the source of all that was good and familiar in their lives? Or me, because I was someone new?

Suzanne led Bella out of the kitchen into the dining room and closed the door. Bella barked once in protest then quieted. Now that she had me all to herself, the puppy offered me enthusiastic play bows and pawed me. For me, it was love at first sight, as I later told Lydia.

Although I can't explain this to anyone who has never had a dog, other dog people understand immediately that each new dog you invite into your life brings with him or her the joy and the memories of her predecessors. I believe a canine spirit exists, a spirit embodied in every dog, connecting us, the humans who love them, to all dogs that have ever been or will be.

These two expressions of "Dog," present that day in Suzanne's kitchen, in Bella and her puppy, confirmed that. I knew instantly that the puppy would offer Lydia and me the love that she carried forward from her forbears, her own unique expression of the canine spirit. As for us, we would be her grateful guardians. The spirit of our much-missed, much-loved Labs hovered over me that day, assuring me that our decision was a fine one, for us and for the puppy.

In the car, the puppy settled down right away in the kennel I'd brought. As we drove home, I talked to her. "Just you wait, little one. You and Lake Paran were made for each other." Lake Paran was a half-mile from our house through the woods. This puppy, like our Labs, was a retriever and a water dog. Like Sally, and Blue, she'd learn to swim and retrieve in the lake.

◦ ◦ ◦

Lydia had already chosen her name. She had been reading about Napoleon and fell hard for Empress Josephine. "Such beautiful skin," she told me, pointing at one of the portraits in the book. "Nice straight nose, don't you think?" The painters couldn't seem to agree on the length of that nose.

"A bit long, though. Maybe this painter wanted to make sure we noticed how straight it is," Lydia laughed. We agreed on one thing, at least: our Josie's nose was very well-shaped and nicely proportioned.

◦ ◦ ◦

Lydia had picked out a few toys and some treats, a collar, and a brush. We could use the leather lead we'd had for years, treated with care and conditioned regularly with saddle soap. Josie sniffed the toys, looked at Lydia, then me, and wagged her tail. "She's very polite, isn't she?" Lydia observed.

We sat at the kitchen table watching Josie explore, following her nose from the kitchen to the living room, to the den, to my study. When she reached the stairs, she set her right foot on the first step, removed it, and sat down, looking at us, "Now what?"

"Suzanne kept a baby gate at the bottom of her stairway," I told Lydia. "I'll bet Josie doesn't know how to go up the stairs. She's not afraid, but she's uncertain. We'll have to teach her." Our Lab puppies had been energetic enthusiasts whose day involved bounding up to and jumping on whatever stood in the way of the next fun thing to do. We had "keep out, keep safe" gates throughout the house. Only after months of training could we allow them free rein in the house.

Josie seemed to know that actions have consequences and that her job was to pay attention and behave appropriately.

She learned to read and interpret cues and adjusted her behavior. Sometimes, hearing an unfamiliar noise, she cocked her head, listening, until she decided whatever it was didn't deserve further attention or comment (a passing car). When someone approached the house, she turned her head toward the front door, panting lightly. Usually, she'd then go to the front hall and sit facing the door waiting for the doorbell to ring. As soon as the visitor entered the house, Josie brought a toy to the front hall, dropped it on the mat there and lay down, ears pricked, her nose inches away from it. If our guest didn't take the hint, she nosed the toy, pushing it this way and that, looking up as if to say, "See? It's easy. Your turn." If that didn't produce the desired result, she picked up the toy and left us.

When I sat in the armchair in my study reading the paper, if Josie wanted my attention, she butted the paper with her nose. I stopped reading, picked up her ball, and played with her.

Lydia reminded me I needed to let Josie know she couldn't always have her way. Soon, a gentle "Not now," was all it took: As soon as she heard the words, she went to the bed I'd placed next to my desk, circled it once or twice, and lay down with a sigh.

By the time Josie was fourteen months old, we took her intelligence, her quickness, for granted. We took her to several obedience classes, which we enjoyed as much as she did. Some days, it seemed all we had to do was think what we wanted her to do. She quickly picked up our cues, enjoyed the challenge, and liked to learn. And, of course, she wanted to please us.

We discovered we had to rein her in when she began to learn some of the basics of agility: Where some of the dogs shied away from climbing the ramp and crossing the platform to the other side, Josie bounded up and ran across, nearly falling off.

At one class, a man with a young black lab came in late and stood beside us at the end of the row. His reply to my greeting was inaudible. His dog sat beside him, head down. Her listless attitude and dull coat made me wonder.

"Is your dog okay?"

"Of course it's okay." He muttered something else.

"Sorry?"

"I mean, a dog like yours isn't really a dog, is it? All fluffed up, like a stuffed animal."

"Poodles are retrievers too, you know."

His face reddened and he tightened up on his dog's choke collar. "Not any more they're not. Now they're just status symbols—pretty, pampered, and hyper."

Sitting beside me, Josie looked at the man, then at me. She stood facing him, leaning against me, panting lightly. I patted her shoulder and took her to another spot in the row. When I glanced back at the man, his Lab was cowering in front of him.

I told Lydia as soon as I got home.

"Did you talk to the trainer?"

"I wanted to talk to you first. I want to be sure not to put her in a tough place."

"Probably she figured out something was wrong. Today was the guy's first day?"

"And from what I can tell, this is his first dog."

"That's a good place to start with the trainer, don't you think? Just tell her he seemed unsure of himself and you were concerned but didn't want to interfere."

As soon as I began to describe the dog and the owner to our trainer, she interrupted me. "That's Joe. The dog is Lily. She's a rescue. I had misgivings, too, so I called the shelter. He had to sign a form agreeing to an inspection visit, which is tomorrow. I'm pretty sure they'll figure this out." She hesitated. "You're right, Randall, the guy doesn't know anything about dogs. He's the one who needs to be trained." Another pause. "And until he is, he shouldn't have a dog."

Having had dogs all my life, it had taken me a while to understand that someone might not know how to be with a dog, how to understand a dog's needs, to appreciate a dog's gifts. Each of ours had taught me something new. Josie, for example, young as she was, had figured out how to tell when I'd reached my limit—cutting wood, say, or hoeing the vegetable garden. She would sidle up and lean against me. The first time, I shooed her away and kept working. She left me alone for five minutes or so. When she came to me again, I knew enough not to scold her. I stopped to consider her behavior, its possible explanation. As I stood there in the garden, puzzling, I realized I felt a little light-headed. And thirsty. So the two of us left the garden and went up to the house for a time out.

The next time, I realized Josie had sensed something in my behavior maybe even in the way I smelled, some clue that something was wrong. I told Lydia, laughing a little at Josie's protective instinct.

"I'm with Josie," Lydia said. "You're due for a check-up, aren't you?"

That's how I found out I had an arrhythmia, something the doctor decided to keep an eye on.

In bed that night, Lydia said, "You're sixty-seven, Randall. Dr. Reade is right. It's time to start taking better care of yourself."

There was no point in stating the obvious: Josie had figured that out first.

o o o

Mud season, spring's dismal preamble, brings cold snaps and warm spells, snow squalls and downpours. Outlanders complain. Vermonters shrug. Today, the smell of mud and pine needles mingled with the steamy fragrance of maple sap drifting up through the woods from a sugar house across the lake. We would soon see snowdrops. And geese, on their way north.

"Spring's in the wings," Lydia said, smiling, reminding me that this aphorism was one my father claimed to have invented.

Every day, rain or shine, Josie and I followed the trail from the foot of the driveway down through the woods to the lake and back.

Today, reading the paper in the living room by the fire, I heard Josie get up from her bed and cross the kitchen floor to the back door, where we hang her lead over the doorknob. Moments later, she came into the living room and dropped the lead in my lap. Three o'clock. Time for our afternoon walk.

Lydia had driven to Burlington early to have lunch with Ellen and Laura. Outside, a few snowflakes floated in circles, as if trying to decide where to land—driveway or woods? I'd read the weather report, which predicted an overcast day and a warming trend. She'd be home by six, in time for dinner, Lydia had promised.

A pot of beef stew sat in the refrigerator with a note: "Put me in the oven at 5 o' clock, 350 degrees." I'd make a salad—Lydia had cut up vegetables, washed lettuce, and made the dressing. We now limited ourselves to dessert once a week, and an occasional glass of wine with dinner. I'd told Lydia she didn't have to cut back on my account. "And drink alone?" We realized then that drinking wine regularly, a custom we'd developed when I was still teaching, had become a habit. And now? "Who needs wine to relax when all you do is relax, all day, every day?"

I let Josie out the back door and put on my jacket and boots. Josie leaped and twirled as she bounded down the driveway. Just past the garage, as soon as she heard the door slam behind me, she stopped and waited. She stood relaxed and quiet while I attached the lead to her collar.

As we headed down the narrow, muddy trail to the lake, I glimpsed patches of snowdrops, green ice-tipped leaves poking up through the snow. Green. The color of hope. The fragrance of boiling maple sap was stronger today.

From the bottom of the trail, where it joined the footpath around the lake, I watched a snow squall sweep down to the far shore, billowing and swirling as it moved out over the ice-covered lake. In the distance, out of sight—behind us? across the lake?—I heard honking, a flock of Canada geese searching for a place to spend the night.

Not far from where we stood, an ice-fishing shanty had sunk up to its roof in the soggy ice. Black blotches of slush and water mottled the lake's surface and pools of water had formed offshore where the geese could ride out the storm overnight. Josie shook her head. Her leather collar swiveled, its buckle jingling against the lead's snap. She flicked her eyes between the footpath and the lake, her tail straight out behind her. Last summer, I often let her loose here, throwing sticks and balls into the lake for her to retrieve. From the beginning, when she had first plunged into the lake, she had been an enthusiastic, strong swimmer

"Cool your jets, kiddo." When I laughed, she looked at me, head cocked, tail sweeping slowly side to side. "Three months, tops, and you'll be swimming again."

As we set out on the footpath, walking clockwise around the lake, the wind began to pick up, shifting in our direction; across the lake, the squall had moved closer, hiding the hills from view.

At the old dock, a quarter of the way around the lake, the geese flew over us as they circled, preparing to land in open water offshore. Josie reared up, barking, knocking me into a stand of pussy willows just off the footpath. I dropped her leash and landed hard, my right ankle twisted, my left leg bent under me. Hand over hand, I pulled myself upright, testing my ankle.

On the bank below me, Josie crouched at the edge of the lake, head up, tail tucked in, nose pointed toward the geese, now paddling in the pool of open water forty, maybe fifty feet away. She slid onto the ice and began to stalk them.

"Josie, stop!"

Gabbling and splashing, the geese eyed her. I shouted again, louder this time. She kept going, her leash dragging behind her. How long before she reached the edge of the pool, before the ice began to break under her?

I slid down the bank and knelt on the slushy ice, gasping as frigid water seeped into my jeans. In waterproof gloves my hands, at least, were warm and dry. Wind-driven snow pellets stung my face. My ankle ached.

"Stop, Josie!" My voice cracked and faded, sucked away by the wind.

She sank down on the ice and looked back, ears cocked.

"Stay!"

As soon as I began to crawl, the lead goose reared upright in the water, beating her wings and paddling as she took off, followed by the rest of the flock, heading away from us.

Josie didn't move.

When I reached her, she thumped her tail and nuzzled me. We were about three feet from the edge of the pool, too close to stand and try to make a run for it. To have any chance of making it back to shore without breaking through the rotting ice, we'd have to stay low—and move slowly.

After removing and pocketing Josie's lead, I slung my left arm over her shoulder, steadied her against me, and pivoted with her until we faced the shore.

Grasping her collar in my left hand, I began to crawl. "Crawl, Josie!"

She looked up, considering. Several months ago, I'd taught her the "army crawl," but we hadn't practiced much since. Would she remember? Would she do it on the wet, slushy ice?

"Josie! Crawl!"

This time, when I tugged her collar, she crouched on all fours and began to move toward the shore as I crawled along beside her. I heard a rumble, felt the ice shudder under us. Josie whined and began to pant. I looked over my shoulder. A liquid shadow crept after us, darkening and widening as the ice began to break up. I felt Josie's shoulders tense and pressed down, as I had at the beginning. "Crawl, Josie!"

I kept my eyes on the clumps of pussy willows ahead of us on the shore where I'd slipped and fallen. We were close now. Twenty feet? Fifteen? The ice was sinking under us. I staggered to my feet, my injured ankle buckling in my boot. Josie scrambled up, clawing her way forward as the ice broke apart and sank and the water began to pool around us.

The water surged up to my neck around my collar and down the front of my jacket, soaking my shirt. My hands were numb. *Keep moving.* I kicked and stroked, pushing against the chunks of ice bobbing and clumping around and into me. Beside me, Josie paddled, watching me.

Where was the bottom?

On this side of the lake, you could walk out into the water until you reached a drop-off, about fifteen or twenty feet from shore, depending on where you entered. I couldn't tell how close we were to the edge of that drop-off. I talked to Josie, encouraging her, my breathing thin and ragged, as my feet sought solid ground. She panted, tossing her head from side to side, as if clearing water from her ears

When she moved closer, pawing at me, I elbowed her away. She came back at me, nosed me once, then again, harder, nudging me to the left, so that I moved left and forward. At last I touched bottom!

I pulled myself up the bank on my stomach. Josie scrambled out of the water, up to the footpath, and shook herself, prancing in place. It had been 40 degrees when we left the house. The water was certainly much colder. I bit down hard to stop my teeth chattering and staggered to my feet.

At the far end of the lake, coming toward us, the geese honked, returning to the pool to ride out the storm. Ragged ice floes bobbed in the channel of dark, choppy water we had left behind.

o o o

It wasn't until we reached the trail through the woods that I felt the pressure in my ears and chest, heard my heart, pounding. I was dizzy. Josie leaned against me, whimpering.

"Home, girl." My voice, barely audible, was a stranger's.

Josie whined.

I cleared my throat. "Home, girl." This time, I sounded more like myself. Josie wagged her tail and started up the trail ahead of me.

o o o

I stripped in the kitchen and piled my wet clothes on the back porch, our mudroom, where we kept our outdoor gear and Josie's towels, beach towels we'd collected over the years for the dogs. The terrycloth robe I often wore in the summer when I went down to the lake for a swim hung on the hook beside the dryer. I slipped it on and took the towels into the kitchen, now steamy with the smell of wet poodle and mud. Josie stood at her dish, gulping water. Her coat hung in stringy mats from head to toe; her legs were covered in mud.

As I began to dry her, I heard the front door open and close. The room spun around me. I sank down on the floor, eyes closed, my arm over Josie's shoulders, forcing myself to breathe, slow, deep, breaths.

"Randall?" Lydia still had her coat and boots on. She sat cross-legged on the floor and took my hand in both of hers. "What happened?"

"She should see the other guy, right Josie?"

Josie pawed me and nuzzled Lydia.

"Just tell me."

"We went for a swim, Josie and I. Since we got back, I've been having a few jumps and bumps ..." I put my hand on my heart, "but otherwise we're fine."

"Save the details for later. First, let's check your heart." She went to find the heart monitor, shedding her coat and kicking off her boots along the way. "And phone Dr. Reade after," she called.

Relief and the comfort of drying Josie, feeling her strong, young muscles, recognizing what she had done to help me find my footing out of the lake, helped calm my heart as I warmed up. I was no longer lightheaded. I was tired, but okay. We were both okay. Considering the temperature of the water and the stress, I was amazed and grateful. Josie was nearly dry. I wanted to get dressed.

Lydia returned with the monitor. We were both surprised at the readings: nearly normal. "I'm going to phone Dr. Reade, anyway," she said. I protested; she shook her head. "My call, Randall. I'll let the vet know too, find out from her what to do about Josie."

Lydia had been in a car crash in high school. The driver, her best friend, had gone through the windshield in the collision and had died, weeks later, of brain damage. She wasn't wearing her seatbelt. Sitting in the front seat, wearing her seatbelt, Lydia escaped with minor bumps and bruises and was clear-headed enough to describe to the State Police and the EMT team what had happened. In their report, they had commended her. "They asked simple questions," she explained. "Just the facts is what they wanted."

I answered her simple questions in simple, short sentences. Just the facts.

"So Josie guided you. She knows that area well. And she knew you were in trouble."

I called Suzanne the next day.

"Did I tell you that Bella was one of a litter of pups the breeder intended to train as service dogs?"

If she had, I didn't remember.

"It turned out that Bella and one of her brothers—there were two females and two males—didn't make the cut. Too sensitive is what they determined from the testing."

"So, Bella was a reject?"

"As a service dog, yes. But they decided to keep her, to breed her—she has a wonderful, solid temperament. Possibly some of her pups would become service dogs, or therapy dogs, is what they thought." Suzanne laughed. "You can see where this story is going, can't you?"

Josie was one of Bella's first litter of four. Only one of those, another female, had gone on to train as a service dog. When the breeder decided to look for another home for Bella, Suzanne had adopted her and Josie.

"I'm getting the picture, yes. Whatever the explanation, Josie saved my life yesterday—and her own. Bella and the rest of us should be proud."

Josie curled up in her bed beside my table while I talked to Suzanne. When I said her name, she came to me and nuzzled my hand.

o o o

The next day, it was nearly 50 degrees at 3 o'clock. "Spring's in the wings," I told Josie as I put on my jacket. Rivulets of snowmelt ran down the street into the storm drain. In the woods, patches of snow gleamed. The leaves of the snowdrops I'd glimpsed yesterday stood above the sodden understory today. Like tiny beacons, a few early buds flashed in the sun.

We paused at the foot of the trail. There was no sign of the geese. Most likely they'd left early, heading to the next stop in their journey north. Ice floes near the shore bobbed and glinted, free at last.

Trying to make sense of the intermittent flashbacks I'd experienced through the night and into the morning, I remembered the theme of an honors course I'd taught several times, "Memory's Minder: The stories we tell." Telling stories is how we make sense of life, I'd told my students. Until we knit them into the fabric of a story that has a beginning, middle, and end, disparate events are as random, and as meaningless, as dust motes dancing in the sun. This story-making impulse is one way we reassure ourselves that our lives have meaning, that what we do matters, a way of seeking closure, by answering questions, to explain ourselves to ourselves. The decisions we make under duress don't make sense until we look back at them, explaining—or justifying—as best we can to ourselves and others why we did what we did.

As soon as I lost my footing and dropped her lead, as soon as Josie plunged in after the geese, I reacted, instinctively, endangering us both. I could spin this into a tale of a daring rescue, of course. Instead, on reflection, I decided to skip the heroics. No bragging rights, here. From now on, when I told the story, I'd emphasize the part where Josie, sensing the lake bottom, saved us both by nudging me in the right direction.

Josie saved the day, not me.

Past Imperfect

1972

Avery and Jo are in bed; it's her mother's bridge night.

In her pajamas, curled up on the couch in the den, Sara is watching the rerun of Perry Mason. Perry has just sent Della to track down information that might prove his client's innocence.

The front door slams. Home late from work, her father greets her on his way to the kitchen.

"I made you a ham sandwich, Dad. It's in the fridge,"

He comes back with a beer and sits beside her.

"Where's the sandwich, Dad?"

"We had pizza at the office." He eyes the TV. "What did I miss?"

"Shhh. This is a good part."

Holding his beer in his left hand, he settles back, kicks his loafers under the coffee table, his right arm stretched out on top of the cushion behind her. He fidgets with the sleeve of her pajama top.

Della returns and hands an envelope to Mason. "He couldn't have done it. He was in Florida," she tells him. "Here's the itinerary."

Attentive to the tension in Della's face as she watches Mason's reaction, Sara squirms. "Stop it, Dad. That tickles."

After moment, the tickling starts again. He fiddles with the hem of her top, slips his fingertips under it and presses the small of her back.

Della points to the page. Mason looks up at the clock. It's time to leave. Now that he has the information, can he win the case?

Sara will never find out.

Shifting his weight, pinning her left leg against the seat cushion, he slides his hand under her top, up her right side, massaging her breast with his fingertips. She twists away from him, off the couch, onto her knees facing the TV.

The show is over.

Her panties are wet.

She pushes away from the table, away from him. Eyes half-shut, he smiles up at her.

"Sleep tight, sweetheart," he calls after her.

o o o

The Fourth of July. Yesterday's sweltering heat and humidity hang over her, a thick, dark cloud. Lying on the floor of her room on the tangled heap of her sheet and blanket, dry-mouthed, she tries to swallow. Had she even slept?

She had been looking forward to the picnic today, to spending the afternoon swimming in her cousins' pool. Not anymore. Why?

She steps into the shower, closes her eyes, lets the cool spray run over her, front and back. She soaps first, beginning with her feet, then scrubs with the washcloth. When she reaches her breasts, her nipples tingle. Her head spins. She grabs the shower curtain. Is she getting sick? Eyes closed, she stands, holding the shower curtain until the spinning stops.

In her room, she picks up her pajamas, panties and a loose, short-sleeved top; they're new, a present from her mother. In the hot weather, she likes how her bare legs feel against the sheets, likes that the top doesn't bunch up during the night. The panties are damp. They smell of pee. Dizzy again, she lies back on her bed. What's wrong with her? Like a bad dream, what happened came back, piecemeal.

The sound of her door opening woke her in the middle of the night. She looked up at him, standing over her in the dark. "Dad? What are you doing? What's going on?"

"Shhh, Sara. Just lie still. Relax."

Kneeling on the floor beside her bed, he lifted her sheet and her pajama top and began to caress her breasts, pinching and pulling her nipples until they tingled.

Blinking back tears, she lay still. For how long, she didn't know. Once again the urge to pee overwhelmed her.

"Sleep tight, sweetheart," he whispered as he closed her door behind him.

Later she will remember that she floated at the pool's deep end until it was time for the picnic, that she held back, sitting as far from him as she could, at the end of the bench, ignoring him when he spoke to her. When her aunt asked what was wrong. "It's getting to be that time of the month." Her father rolled his eyes.

He didn't come that night, or the one after that. A week went by. She didn't fall asleep until the sky began to brighten, listening for his footsteps, for the sound of her door opening. In the morning, her mother asked what was wrong, "Bad dream," she lied. The next night, it happened again.

Sometimes he came to her after he'd been drinking, late at night, watching TV. Sometimes he came in the middle of the night. She never knew if or when he would appear beside her bed, whispering to her, "relax, just lie still." She lay rigid, eyes squeezed shut, trying to imagine a way out. What if she ran away? What if she took her Girl Scout knife to bed with her, threatened him? What if she stabbed him? What if she screamed? The morning after, she delayed going downstairs for breakfast, waiting until he left for work.

One day in November, Sara woke feeling that something had changed. That she was different somehow. She closed her eyes and took a deep breath, feeling her lungs expand as she drifted into the vast space that opened within her, a space she felt she must protect. This is how she described it to herself then. How it came to be, or where it came from, she couldn't say. How she could protect it, she had no idea, but she knew when the time came, she would know what to do. She was no longer afraid.

A week after Thanksgiving, she woke when she heard the doorknob turn. When he came in, she pretended to be asleep. He drew back the blanket. She held her breath. Suddenly she was looking down at herself, watching him lift her sheet, then her nightgown. She heard her own voice, her normal speaking voice, clear and calm. "I'll tell Mom."

He straightened up. She braced herself, holding the sheet tight against her. All she could see was his shape, looming over her in the dark. As he turned away, toward the open door and the nightlight in the hall, she saw his face. He was grinning.

"How did you sleep?" he asked the next morning. Her mother, Avery, and Jo looked at her, as if her answer were the key to something important, something that would change their lives forever.

"Okay, I guess."

"I thought I heard you talking. Maybe you were having a bad dream?"

A bad dream. Now she knew. That's what he'd say if she told her mother.

She looked down at her cereal bowl, at the slices of banana partially submerged in the milk, surrounded by cornflakes. "I had a nightmare, the kind that makes you believe you're awake."

"Probably the weather." He nodded. "Just before a big storm, I have bad dreams, too. Well, it's supposed to snow today. We'll all sleep better tonight."

For years, Sara sometimes lay awake until early morning, waiting, heart pounding. He never again came to her in the night.

o o o

1979

The year after they graduated from college, Sara and her college roommate, Emma, both found jobs in Newport, Rhode Island. Emma taught French at St. George's School; Sara was the copy editor for a sailing magazine. Three years later, when Ames & Jones offered her a job as associate editor in their Boston office, she accepted, although she knew the possibility of finding an affordable place to live anywhere near Boston was slight. "If you commute from Newport, you'll have plenty of time to read more of those Russian novels you like so much," Emma suggested.

"More likely I'll be vetting proposals." Sara shook her head. "Twelve-hour workdays including the commute? Too much like a perpetual cram week."

"You could get lucky and find a place in Fall River."

"Which reduces the commute by forty-five minutes, maybe? I might as well stay in Newport." Sara laughed. "I have an orientation meeting next week with my editor. I'll see if she has any ideas about local rentals."

Three days into her search, thanks to a tip from the human resources manager at Ames & Jones, Sara found the apartment on Beacon Street, between Arlington and Berkeley, five blocks from her office.

In the middle of a block of 19th-century brick townhouses in Boston's Back Bay, the building had been subdivided into ten apartments, most of them owner-occupied. Her apartment was on the fourth floor, at the back overlooking a large oak tree and the alley—four hundred square feet, one bedroom with a walk-in closet, a living room/dining alcove, kitchen, and bath. It was minuscule. "It's perfect," Sara told Emma. "Make that almost perfect. It's a walk-up.

But there are two big windows—one in living room, the other in in the bedroom."

"Off-street parking and storage space?"

"Neither. I'll worry about that when I'm promoted to publisher."

"St. Joseph was looking out for you," Emma teased. "Louise is still hunting. After six months she hasn't found anything she can afford."

"As to that—affordability, I mean—it'll be chicken noodle soup and peanut butter sandwiches—or starve."

"You'll save on the commute, anyway. And you survived Paris, don't forget."

The summer after graduation, they had spent a month in a studio apartment on the Left Bank. On the fifth floor, it had a living room with a fold-out couch, an alcove with a double bed, a bathroom, and a "kitchen-in-a-closet." The best part: It was within walking distance of Notre-Dame, the Louvre, the Musée d'Orsay, the Musée de Cluny, the Orangerie, the Jardin des Plantes, and the Jardin de Luxembourg. They had taken the Métro once, to the Musée Marmottan, to see the Monet exhibition.

They learned that a roast chicken, a pot of soup, or a casserole lasted almost a week if they were careful. Wednesdays, they finished the baguette they bought on Monday, having discovered that a chunk of aging baguette, warmed in the oven, spread with butter and jam, was nearly as good as a fresh croissant dunked in café au lait. At the end of their first week, the greengrocer on the corner gave them a discount on fruits and vegetables—pears and plums, green beans, carrots—at or nearing the end of their shelf-life.

"That part will be like Paris," Sara agreed. "Charles Street is four blocks away. I can shop there the way we did in France. I doubt I'll get a mark-down on fruits and veggies, but at least I can buy single portions at the deli." She laughed. "I can sleep late and walk to work." The Ames & Jones office was five blocks away.

"So you can window shop and people watch when you get bored."

"Let's see how the job goes before I start thinking about what to do when I'm bored."

o o o

The week she moved into the apartment, Sara painted the living room and dining alcove—neither had been painted in ten years, the landlord told her. He accepted her offer to do the job herself and paid for the materials. (He had also provided a stepladder and step stool). At last her furniture (couch, end tables, lamps) was in place, and she had hung her three Bokhara rugs on the wall across from the couch. Today she'll start on the bedroom and closet, painted shocking pink by the previous tenant.

After washing the walls and woodwork, depending on how fast everything dries, she should be able to begin painting tomorrow. The paint cans, the stirrers, her gloves, the tape, rollers, and brushes are stacked in the corner. A layer of newspaper covers the floor. She wants to finish by midweek at the latest so she can spend next weekend in Newport with Emma.

They had bought a two-person kayak three years ago, when Sara lived there. On weekends and days off during the summer, they paddled out to Rose Island for a picnic lunch, watching the the J-Boats and smaller sailboats heading north or south under the Newport Bridge. She was looking forward to a weekend away, her reward for finishing this project and likely her last kayak outing until next spring.

She moves the stepstool inside the closet, under the shelves, where she has stacked six boxes. Removing them will be the easy part, she knows. The hard part—inventorying and dividing up the contents—could take several days.

Neither Avery, living in Paris now, nor Jo, in D.C., knows about the boxes. Neither knows their mother had saved the photos, papers, letters, and other memorabilia over the years, planning eventually to give each of them a chance to go through the collection and find the pieces they each wanted to keep. When she moved to California, she had left the boxes with Sara, telling her to decide what to do with them.

o o o

After Emma left, Sara stored the photographs for Avery and Jo in zip-lock bags and boxed them, with their letters, report cards, Avery's swimming medals, and Jo's seventh-grade diary. On top of her own pile lay the packet of letters she had sent from Nice. She had arrived on July 1 and left on August 5, 1975. There were twenty-five letters, including the ones from her week in Paris. Not quite one a day. She sat at the dining table with a cup of tea, five weeks of aerogrammes arrayed in front of her. What was she looking for? Would she even recognize herself?

Postmarked Paris, the first described the house and village near Fontainebleau where she stayed with her mother's friend, Vivi, the week after she arrived. She closed her eyes, remembering the horse-drawn cart that passed by her window every morning, the heavy, lavender-scented linen sheets, the old stone house that smelled of wood smoke and sandalwood, escargots for dinner, *"a piece of buttery, garlicky rubber (ick!)."*

The two letters about sightseeing in Paris listed the landmarks (dutifully she had named all the important ones, even ones they hadn't visited). The one about her lunch with Vivi at the café on the Champs-Elysées, enthused *"… the best toasted cheese sandwich ever, but the exhaust and cigarette smoke made me cough and sneeze so much, I couldn't finish it."* She hadn't mentioned the man sitting across from them, who stared at her, taking long, deep drags on his cigarette, sipping his espresso. Vivi caught her eye, smiled, and turned her head, gazing out at the passersby. So did Sara.

From then on, she paid attention to how French women behaved when a man looked at them, following them with his eyes as they passed on the street or sat in a café. In the café, like Vivi, they turned their heads, sometimes checking their watch, sometimes opening a book or a newspaper. On the street, chins lifted, they looked straight ahead, unsmiling. From then on, if a man tried to catch her eye, she focused on a distant shop window as though on her way to meet someone.

Too excited to sleep on the overnight train from Paris to Nice, which stopped and started often, Sara lay on her stomach on the top bunk looking out the window in the corridor at the night sky, watching the flicker of lights as they passed by villages and towns. In the countryside, because it was a clear, moonless night, she looked up at Orion and the Pleiades, imagining herself at home on a summer night like this one, on her back in the grass, these familiar constellations and others filling the sky above the tree line, the fireflies' intermittent flashes above the garden.

When they reached the coast before seven the next morning, travelling along the track overlooking the calm, blue sea, people were already out working in their gardens behind their cottages, most of them stone or stucco with tile roofs. Ruffles of red or pink bougainvillea festooned the walls. On some of them, fishing nets hung on hooks, drying in the sun.

The fragrance of wild thyme, laurel, lavender, and bay drifted in from recently mowed fields.

In Nice, just off the Boulevard Cimiez, the marble, colonnaded villa looked nothing like the brick or stucco college dormitories she knew. Abandoned in WWII, the villa had been refurbished by the city and converted into a boarding school after the war.

The former salon, now the dining room, opened to a walled garden of flowering shrubs and fruit trees, and four massive cypress trees standing like sentinels at each corner. The dorm rooms, doubles for the most part, on the second, third, and fourth floors, ran the length of dimly lit marble corridors. Standing at one end of the second-floor corridor, you could whisper and the person standing at the opposite end could hear every word. The eight-foot windows in each room had slatted shutters, but no screens. At night, Sara's roommate, Françoise, insisted on keeping the shutters closed. Even so, mosquitoes found their way in. The mosquito repellant Sara had brought was useless, but *citronelle*, worked.

The day after she arrived, Sara learned to say, "I'm homesick," in French. She was only a little homesick, really. She met a few of the other Americans on her floor, most of them Juilliard students, as well as some of the French students, who spoke a little English. At registration, she learned she was the youngest in her group of ten, the only American, and the only one who hadn't studied with Mme Schreiber at the conservatory. Sleepless the night before the first class, she wrote, "*I'm glad I didn't know about the other students ahead of time. I would have been too intimidated to come.*"

At the end of the first week, she sent a birthday card to Jo: "*I am still 'me' but being here makes it possible to begin to be 'me being here'. My hair is longer and a bit sun-streaked, and I'm getting a tan (at least my face and my arms).*" She had stepped into a new role, making up her lines as she went along. The more French she spoke, the more she heard herself speaking French, the more she felt she was fitting in, that her transformation was real. She was Sara, an American in Nice, learning to speak French, studying the gestures the French used, imitating their tone of voice. And smiling less. Françoise told her Americans smile too much. You couldn't trust them. When Sara asked why, she shrugged. "No one smiles that much, unless they're trying to take advantage of you."

At breakfast, pigeons sauntered into the dining room from the garden, heads bobbing, as they searched for breadcrumbs under the tables, sometimes brushing against her bare legs. For breakfast, there were pitchers of coffee and steamed milk, and sliced baguettes, with plum jam and butter. Served in heavy white pottery bowls, the jam was made from plums from the garden.

Re-reading her letters, Sara visualizes the long tables with their heavy, white linen tablecloths, the black and white tile floor. She can hear the pigeons cooing and the flutter of their wings as they move around the dining room, smell the fragrance of the ripe plums in the trees, feel the crunch of the bread crust and the smooth tangy jam on her tongue.

o o o

In her early fifties, Madame Schreiber wore her blond hair in a chignon, spoke English and French with a German accent, and called Sara "ma petite." (She called the students who worked with her at the conservatory, "Monsieur," or "Mademoiselle.") Each day, five students performed a selection from their repertoire. Jean played selections from Bartok's "Microcosmos." Joelle was working on Schubert's "Impromptus." Robert and Nicole played selections from Brahms' "Intermezzos." After each performance, Madame solicited comments and suggestions from the rest of the class, then added her own.

At first, as the youngest, least advanced student—the only American—Sara was reluctant to speak up. With a wave of her hand and a smile, Madame reassured her: "Go right ahead, Sara. I'll translate." Within a few days, Sara caught on: She would say something positive, an overview, in English, then suggest changes in the dynamics or the tempo.

Thursday morning before her first performance, Sara woke with a knot in her stomach. At breakfast, she drank some coffee, but she couldn't eat. Even the pigeons, fluttering in and out of the room, seemed agitated. At nine, when she arrived at the studio, the chairs had been set up in a semi-circle, as usual. At the piano, Madame and Robert were reviewing a fingering problem in one of the Intermezzos. Madame turned and greeted her warmly. Robert nodded at her. Sara removed her sweater, draped it over the back of the chair, and sat, holding the score in her lap.

Once everyone had settled, Madame took her customary seat next to the piano and smiled at Sara, who stood and announced the pieces she would play, then sat and adjusted the height of the music bench. She reached into the pocket of her slacks and took out the lace-edged cotton batiste handkerchief, a gift from her piano teacher, whose voice she heard: "Take a deep breath, wipe your hands, each finger, and then the keyboard. This will help calm your nerves. If your hands are trembling, by the time you finish you'll be fine." Her hands trembled to such an extent she wasn't sure she would be able to play a single note, let alone remember the pieces she had chosen, a Bach prelude and fugue. And yet, she did remember, thanks to muscle memory. When she finished, Madame clapped softly. "Brava, Sara." She turned to the others, waiting for their comments.

Mostly, the other students were kind to one another, their comments constructive. There was one girl named Genevieve, who was tough on everyone. She leaned back after Sara finished, legs outstretched, arms crossed, glowering. (She sat by herself and chain smoked during their breaks.) As soon as Sara finished, she spoke up in English: "Practice the fugue with a metronome. Your tempos are all over the place. And you need more flow in the prelude, more legato."

Jacqueline, the girl next to Genevieve, shook her head. "I disagree with Genevieve. Your tempo is okay for now and the legato is developing nicely. Once the notes are in your fingers, you'll be fine." Genevieve frowned and looked down at her hands, folded in her lap. Sara thanked her—this was protocol. Jacqueline, her defender, smiled at her. After class, she joined Sara on the walk back to the dormitory. "Genevieve is a perfectionist—about her own work and everyone else's. Don't take her comments too seriously. Listen to Madame. She's why we're here, after all."

From then on, before each class, Sara reminded herself that the students' role as a group was to provide one another daily experience playing for others. She also told herself the other students, like her, were students first. Including Genevieve.

The window in her practice room overlooked the conservatory garden through the fronds of an ancient date palm, which rustled in the breeze, sometimes tapping the walls and the window. The piano, a battered Pleyel upright, had several sticky keys. When Sara reported the problem, the program assistant in charge of housekeeping details assured her the technician would fix them as soon as he could. He showed up three weeks later, the day before her recital, three days before she left.

Judy, a Juilliard student who had attended the conservatory the year before, had the room across from Sara and Françoise. When Sara asked about the cold showers and the screenless windows, she laughed. "C'est la vie! Pretend you're at camp, on a lake in Vermont. You'll get used to it. Besides, it'll be over before you know it. And be glad it's not January." She looked at Sara. "You know, there's no central heating."

Of course, she ran out of spending money. When she and her mother planned her budget, they hadn't considered the cost of the bus to and from the beach, or the extras. The first time she went to the beach, Sara saw that she was the only woman wearing a one-piece. *"People stared,"* she wrote to Jo. *"It was like wearing a sign: 'I am American.'"* So she bought a bikini and threw out the one piece. That made the first large dent in her budget. And she couldn't pass the patisserie on the way to and from the bus stop without buying a macaron or a madeleine. Also, she bought drinks and chips for her friends at the café after the evening concerts. Swearing Jo to secrecy, and promising to bring her a special gift, she had asked her to make sure her mother sent her $100 to tide her over. "Do NOT tell Dad."

Her mother sent the check right away.

When Sara reads the letter about her conversation class, she smiles: *"Alain Duclos. Very shy. Very cute. He wears his hair longish, parted on the left side, and when he makes a point, or corrects one of us, he smiles—not making fun of us, but encouraging us to pay attention. He is not at all demanding or professorial. He can't look us in the eye when he speaks to us—there are five of us, all women. I'm the only American. And the youngest. He asks us questions—the usual small talk: 'Where are you from?' 'Where do you go to school?' 'What is your favorite book?' We're reading a book called 'Le Grand Meaulnes.' It's when he starts talking about it, answering our questions, he lights up. He leans forward, as if trying to pour his ideas and excitement into us. I think I learn more French that way—it's as though his enthusiasm itself breaks down the language barrier."*

She had seen him the first time on the way to the beach her first week. Seated on the benches in the middle of the bus, they couldn't avoid looking at one another. The first time their eyes met, he averted his gaze. The second time, she did. Both laughed. He blushed. He got off at the stop before hers. The following Monday, at the first conversation class, he had nodded and smiled at her when she came in a few minutes late, as if sharing a private joke. No one else seemed to notice.

He came to all the evening concerts at the Arènes on a hilltop above the city, joining a group of students at the café afterwards. Often, he stayed on with her after the others left, telling her stories about the Sorbonne and his apprehension about spending the next year teaching French in England. "It's not just that the food is terrible. Although it certainly is that," he frowned. "I want to work on my own writing. I worry I won't have time." He had laughed at himself then. "I'm just getting started. Short stories about my grandparents and their life in Périgord, before they moved to Paris." He shrugged. "I love to read. Writing? That's another story." He laughed again. This time at his own pun.

At their café table on the edge of the Arènes, looking down at the

Promenade des Anglais and the *baie des anges*, he had introduced her to Pernod and unfiltered Gauloises cigarettes.

"Why is it called *la baie des anges*?" she wanted to know.

"It's named for a small shark that used to live in the bay, a shark with fins that resemble wings." He smiled. "It's a pretty story. Another story tells how angels brought Adam and Eve here after they were thrown out of Eden." He sipped his drink, looking at her over the top of his glass. "I like both stories, don't you? So often, the answer to a 'why question' leaves plenty of room for different explanations, even contradictory ones, all somewhat plausible. I like to imagine all the people over the years who've heard the stories, who believed them simply because they are good stories." He laughed. "Who cares what's true?"

"I like the one about the shark best," Sara said.

Alain sipped his drink. "So do I."

They usually spoke English. He told her he needed the practice for his work at the school in England. He had explained to her he preferred the American accent, "because it is softer, less pinched," that she was helping him to adjust his pronunciation. "My professors at the Sorbonne would be horrified, of course."

"What will your students in England think, I wonder?"

"Fortunately for me, since I'm their teacher, I'll do it my way."

"And if your headmaster doesn't like your American way?"

"I'm French. I'm a good negotiator. We'll sort it out. I'll offer him a bottle of good Bordeaux to look the other way."

Judy caught sight of them one evening, sitting at their usual corner table at the café. Later, back in the dorm, she'd teased Sara, "Looks like our French teacher has a crush on you, Sara."

"Me? We're just friends. Besides, he's way too old for me."

"You're sixteen. He's twenty-two. He's not too old." Judy looked at her. "He's certainly not old enough to be your father," she added.

Sleepless that night, Sara thought about Judy's comment. "He's not old enough to be your father," she'd said. Sara had broken up with her boyfriend her freshman year in high school, when he touched her breast. She hadn't had a steady relationship with a boy her own age since then. But Alain was different. He didn't touch her except to hold her hand as he lit her cigarette, or to take her arm crossing the street as they walked back to the villa together.

During the last two weeks of the program, they saw each other every day, as usual, for their class, and after the evening concerts, they met at the café. The weekend before she left, he took her out to dinner.

"I want to write to you," he told her as they walked home. "May I?"

"Of course," Sara laughed. "But you'll have to tell me all your stories."

"Even the ones that aren't true?"

"Those, especially." Sara looked at him. "I won't know the difference." They both laughed.

That night at the door, he put his arms around her and kissed her on both cheeks. An affectionate—and formal—goodbye.

Did Alain remember those evenings, Sara wondered? Now thirty-one, had he married? Did he have children? Of course, she had had a crush on him. But she had been too young in a way that had nothing at all to do with their age difference. In her time in Nice, she had begun to heal, and to reclaim her physical and emotional self in the process of adapting to being in France, being who she was in France, immersed in an experience that helped her change, to leave behind the trauma, to step out from under its shadow into a different light. Every day she had taken in the sights, sounds, and smells around her, away from horror, into confidence in her power to heal herself.

o o o

Near the end of her five weeks in Nice, Sara had felt as though a piece of music she had been struggling with had finally become her own, that it was, at last, a part of her. On the bus to the beach on her next to last day, she watched her reflection in the window, observing herself as if she were a stranger, someone she looked forward to getting to know. At the beach, she found a perfectly round stone. She held it in the palm of her hand, absorbing its warmth.

When she arrived at the airport, the moment she saw her father their eyes locked. Sara lifted her chin and turned her head.

o o o

A month later, waking in the night, clasping the stone over her heart, she closed her eyes, heard the cart passing her window in the house near Fontainebleau, heard the echo of her own footsteps in the corridors of the dormitory, and recalled the play of light on the *baie des anges* under the cloudless sky.

Hermit Crabs

Bellied up to the sink, Ellis peers into the mirror, positions the razor on his left cheekbone and draws it down over his jaw. He can do this blindfolded, he's told her, although he hasn't, to her knowledge, ever tried. Daily for twenty years, he has performed this task. No mustache. No beard. Not Ellis.

Lying on her side in their bed, watching him, Kate considers the irony: Ellis's shaving ritual, which wakes her each morning, is as reliable a feature of his life as his punctual departure for his office at 8:30 and the precision displayed in his drawings. As he often reminds her, in architecture small mistakes (scaling errors, for example) add up to big trouble (lawsuits).

Her routine differs from his in the myriad disruptions that occur daily. Managing Melanie and Josh means planning their day and having a back-up plan. During the school year, alert to their moods and needs, even when they're at school, Kate watches the clock, imagining where they are and what they are doing throughout the school day: Will Melanie, eight, speak up in her math class when she knows the answer? Will Josh, four, settle down at quiet time?

She rolls onto her back, following the shadow of the branches outside her window moving across the ceiling. A memory floats among them: She is four, standing beside her father, imitating his gestures as he shaves. The mirror over the sink shimmers with steam.

He finishes and crouches beside her, wiping her face with a washcloth, warming her cheek. Feel the warmth.

Kate touches her face.

"Honey?" Ellis kneels beside the bed. "Kate?"

Eyes shut, she lies still. She feels his weight shift against the bed as he leans in to kiss her cheek. Old Spice and peppermint. Feel the warmth. "Another day at the races," he whispers in her ear.

o o o

In the kitchen Ellis stands at the stove, ladle in hand, an apron bunched around his waist, watching two eggs immersed in boiling water. The timer goes off. Sunlight streams across the floor, creating ripples of shadow in the rough French tiles.

Ellis wraps a potholder around the saucepan's handle and lifts it from the stove in one smooth motion. He stops midway across the kitchen, looking at Kate standing in the doorway. "What's the matter?"

Kate gestures at the beach towels and bag next to the backdoor. "We're not going to the beach today."

Ellis checks the calendar on the refrigerator door. Melanie had made the flip calendar at school, each page marked off in equal squares. "July 11," Ellis reads, "'Mia, 8:30, beach, TBC.' Your handwriting. Melanie must have seen the note. What's 'TBC'?"

"'To be confirmed.' Mia and I talked about this a while ago, before she and Dad came down." Mia and her father had rented a house in Westport for the month of July. "I penciled in the date and time. I expected her to confirm." Kate shrugs. "The problem is the greenheads. At this time of year, it's a day-to-day thing, depending on the wind, the heat." Ignoring Ellis's raised eyebrows, Kate opens the cupboard and takes out Cheerios for Melanie, Rice Krispies for Josh. She closes the door and faces Ellis. How could she have forgotten?

"8:30 is early. They should be fine." Ellis sets his two slices of toast and the eggs on the table, butters the toast, cuts it into triangles, scoops out the eggs and divides them evenly, one egg per slice. He's an architect, after all. "Ask Mia to bring them home by eleven, just to be sure." He forks a piece of toast and egg into his mouth. "Or you can call it off."

In her nightgown, hair tousled, Polly comes into the kitchen. She picks up Melanie's brush from the "Hold Everything" basket on the counter and tugs it through her hair, grimacing when it catches on a snarl. "Call what off?"

"A beach date I made, with Mia—for Mia and the kids, I mean. It's today. I forgot."

"Mommy brain?" Polly twirls a finger around her head. "Why don't I go with them? One adult per kid evens the odds, right?"

Ellis chuckles. "You? An adult?"

"I'm their aunt. Besides, I'm only two years younger than Kate. So, yeah, I guess I qualify." Polly and Ellis laugh.

"The greenheads have started," Kate interjects.

"Ugh. I'll pass." Polly shudders.

"Good on you. Because my to-do list requires your assistance. Ann Taylor? Shopping for a dress for the Club party? You agreed to stay with Josh and Mel. Thanks to Mia, you get to shop with me instead."

Ellis puts down his fork and stands to clear his plate. "Or I could come home early so you can go over to Newport before dinner."

It's an hour's drive each way to Newport from Tiverton. They'd need at least three hours. After ten years, Ellis still has no idea how much time it might take Kate to find a dress she likes. "Let's stick with Plan A. Since we won't have the kids, we won't have to hurry."

Kate pours a glass of orange juice for everyone except Josh. Until Mia had served him chocolate milk for lunch recently, he'd always accepted orange juice for breakfast. Now, when Kate offers him juice, he glowers. She hasn't forced the issue, in the hope he will come around on his own.

The front door opens and slams. Josh skids across the kitchen floor, nearly colliding with the table. Kate grabs him. "Mia's here, Mom!" He pushes away from her, sliding into Ellis's arms, "Dad, Mia's here!"

"Breakfast first, kiddo," Ellis lifts him, nuzzles his forehead, and puts him on his high stool by the counter. Leaning over him, pouring his milk, his shoulder blades firm and warm against her, Kate inhales the corn-silk sweetness rising from the top of his head. Ellis smiles at Kate. They ignore Josh's slurps.

Kate checks the beach bag. She knows Melanie has remembered everything, even the red shovel that Josh takes everywhere. So why does she bother? Because this is what she does best? Because she must be certain she has provided everything herself before they venture forth? Even with Mia? At the sound of the car door slamming, Kate watches Melanie and Mia hoist Josh's car seat into Mia's Volvo.

Especially with Mia.

o o o

After their parents' divorce, before their father and Mia married, Kate and Polly often spent the night at his apartment. Sometimes he had an early class and Mia gave them breakfast and took them to school. One time, she had dropped the quart of milk she'd just removed from the fridge, splattering them all. Another time, as Mia struggled to brush Polly's hair—fine, curly, easily snarled—Polly protested. "Kate! Kati-e-e-e-e!"

As soon as Kate appeared, Polly stopped crying and held out the brush to her. Mia sat on the edge of the tub, hands clasped tight between her knees, shoulders hunched, looking at the floor.

Mia was afraid of them, Kate realized then. And trying too hard, she knows now.

o o o

Kate pushes her bangs away from her forehead with one hand and holds her hair off her neck with the other. She looks at her neck and upper chest in the fitting room mirror. The freckles she's acquired make the case: Only sleeves and a high neckline will do. In the fitting room, she takes the navy-blue linen shift off the rack behind her, eyeing the rumpled skirt. The first dress she saw on the sale rack, it has a boat neck and elbow-length sleeves. The style, such as it is, is fine.

"Linen," she sighs, as Polly enters the fitting room with three dresses. Linen wrinkles; that's that. But people notice, even though they pretend not to mind the wrinkled skirt, jacket, or dress. Kate refuses to be the object of such scrutiny, the disapproval it implies.

"I suppose I can always dry-clean it every time I wear it."

"It's perfect." Polly's eyes narrow. "For a funeral."

"Polly, please. It's my job. My role. I have to pay attention to this stuff. The kids, too. Or people talk." Polly makes light of others' expectations. She doesn't care that here, in this small community, being the wife of an up-and-coming architect is like living in a glass house (Ellis jokes that he'll build her a windowless house). She dismisses the idea that Kate's behavior and her appearance can help or harm Ellis's reputation.

Barefoot and down to bra and panties, Kate eyes the outfit she put on that morning: khaki twill L. L. Bean A-line skirt, lime-green cotton Lacoste T-shirt, Coach leather scuffs. It's the same outfit she wears daily. Because it's neat, practical, and neutral. No one can find fault with that. Except Polly and her mother, who had told her she looked dowdy.

Polly favors bright colors, mixed or matched, and accessorized with wooden beads and copper bracelets from places like Vietnam or Chile. Kate accepts this. She even admires Polly's offbeat style. But she could never make it her own. Polly hangs three dresses on the rack.

"This won't hurt a bit. I promise." Polly motions at the mirror. She holds an iridescent green sheath up to Kate's shoulder and watches Kate's eyes hover, then dart away.

"Too shiny, too sexy."

Polly hangs up the dress and takes down a purple A-line with three-quarter sleeves and a V-neck. She smiles into the mirror. "Just try it."

"No way." Kate shudders.

Polly's third selection, a maroon silk sheath, has a scoop neck and short sleeves. She holds the skirt to Kate's cheek. Against the lustrous silk, Kate's brown eyes flash, her dark hair gleams. She frowns.

"Now what?"

Kate pokes at the neckline, pulls at a sleeve. "My neck is too scrawny. And I'm so freckled. Plus my upper arms are flabby. It's just not me. I'm a thirty-five-year-old mom, not arm candy."

"Come on, Kate. Just try it."

Kate looks at her watch. They've been here an hour. Ten more minutes. If she doesn't find something, she'll wear the dress she has at home. Made of pale green polished cotton, she had worn it to a wedding a year ago. Nearly new, she thinks. Why spend money on another dress I may wear only once?

"Turn around, would you?" Polly slides the dress over Kate's head and zips it up. "Now you can look."

"Oh, Polly."

She remembers a shopping trip with Mia, not long after Mia and her father had married. She had just turned fourteen. Mia had picked A-line skirts and button-less cardigans in clear, bright pastels, pointing out to her how she could mix and match them so she wouldn't get bored wearing the same outfit, day after day.

Mia thought about style. Her mother thought about durability.

Kate had tried to see herself through Mia's eyes, trying on Mia's approval with each new outfit. It hadn't worked. At home, at her mother's house, she had hidden the clothes in the back of her closet where they stayed until her mother discovered them, their tags still attached, and gave them away to Goodwill.

And now?

Who is the alluring, 35-year-old woman looking back at her? Kate is a wife. And a mom. That's the way she and her friends talk about themselves. "Just a mom," they say, laughing lightly, when they meet someone new. The person in the mirror, Kate tells herself, is someone I'd like to know better.

"Katie?"

Kate turns back to Polly. "I'll take it. It's perfect for the party." Even her voice sounds different, as warm and eager as the play of light across the glossy silk.

○ ○ ○

On the way to Horseneck Beach, Mia reviews her checklist: cell phone, beach blanket, towels, cooler, sunscreen. And First Aid kit. When Kate had asked if she had one, Mia had reached into the car and pulled it out of her beach bag. "It's brand new."

Kate had smiled, and nodded, but her downcast eyes cancelled out the smile. "Stay with Mia by the tide pools, Josh." Kate reached across Josh to buckle Melanie's seatbelt and closed the door. She'd turned to Mia, avoiding her eyes, attempting a casual tone. "You know about the greenheads?"

"I read the article in the paper yesterday."

"Keep an eye on the wind. If it shifts—from east to west—head home." Kate looked up into the cloudless sky. "Anyway, by eleven or so, the kids will have had enough sun."

"Me, too," Mia said.

○ ○ ○

At the foot of the driveway, Mia looks in her side mirror. Arms crossed, eyes wide, Kate stands by the front steps, watching the car. *Let's go, Kate. Give me a chance.*

At the turnoff to the beach, Mia glances in the rearview mirror.

In his car seat, Josh examines the Day-Glo orange pail and the green shovel she has bought him. His white-blond cowlick bobs gently in the draft from her window. Leaning back, Melanie looks out her window.

Nine o'clock. The parking lot is nearly empty. Puffs of exhaust emerge from the tail pipe as Mia downshifts. There are a few joggers on the beach, a couple of wind surfers out beyond the surf line. No swimmers yet. The knot in her stomach relaxes. So far, so good.

She parks the Volvo near some beach plums and leaves the windows ajar. Josh carries his pail and shovel, his beach towel draped around his neck; Melanie slides the beach bag strap over her shoulder, gripping the bottom of the bag, and makes her way along the path, head down. Mia follows, scanning the beach ahead for a place to settle.

As soon as he steps onto the beach, Josh drops his beach towel and spins around, grinning. "Can I go see the hermits?"

"Sunscreen first, Josh." As Mia smooths the cream over his neck and shoulders. Josh squirms just enough to let her know he's controlling his impatience, tolerating the delay. The cream is a greasy combination of sunscreen and insect repellent, the recommended defense against the greenheads. Mia takes private satisfaction in having prepared so well. She makes a mental note to tell Kate about her discovery of the greenhead repellent—it's new, invented by someone who lives in the northeast, and summers on these beaches.

Free at last, hugging pail and shovel to his chest, Josh runs toward the tide pools, yelling, "Here I come, hermits."

"Mom makes him wait for her," Melanie tells Mia, watching Josh, eyeing Mia.

"On my way." Mia pats her shoulder. "I'll come help with your castle in a while."

o o o

Formed of clusters of boulders at the north end of Horseneck Beach, the tide pools fill and drain daily, some of them slower than others. Their bottoms strewn with gravel, shells, and seaweed, they shelter clams, mussels, and hermit crabs.

Now, Josh checks them all, seeking the one with the most hermit crabs, scrambling back and forth on mysterious missions. Top-heavy in their periwinkle shells, they fold their legs and disappear at the first hint of danger.

Cloud shadows skim the water's surface, weightless as the ease that settles light as mist on Mia's shoulders. A Frisbee flashes back and forth between two teenagers up the beach near where Melanie has begun to build a sandcastle.

Josh kneels in the pool, picks up a hermit crab, holds it upside down, its legs wriggling. He giggles. Mia grins at him.

A little after 10 o'clock, it's time for a snack. Mia settles the kids on the blanket. Melanie takes three juice cartons and plums from her beach bag. Cross-legged, Josh holds out his hand. "Two crackers, Mia."

"Please, Mia," says Melanie.

"Please, Mia," Josh says under his breath.

"Let's see how much sand we won't eat today." Mia wipes their hands with a damp paper towel and hands them each two crackers and a slice of apple.

Beyond the sandbar, the water flattens and calms; there are now six Frisbee players flipping the disk to one another across and around a wide circle; an orange-tailed blue kite swoops lazily overhead. The breeze is dying. The wind surfers are paddling in. Both kids' shoulders are pink. Sunscreen or no, Mia knows they'll have to leave soon.

As she considers how best to present this idea—a stop for ice cream on the way home?—Mia sees the first greenhead. More appear, darting around them. They're not interested in the food. They're after blood. One lands on Melanie's arm, another on her cheek.

"Ow." Melanie bites her lip.

Mia wraps a towel around her, swatting at several greenheads circling around them. So much for the repellent. New and useless. Snapping open the First Aid kit, she tears the antiseptic packet and places the pad on the sting swelling on Melanie's arm. "Just hold on like this, okay? We'll put ice on it when we get home." Mia hugs her.

Melanie sniffles. "You can go help Josh if you want."

"Did you see where he went?"

Melanie shakes her head.

He had been there a minute ago, huddled under the towel, now lying in a heap beside the beach bag. Had the greenheads scared him away?

"Maybe he's at the tide pool," Mia says, hoping Melanie can't hear the fear in her voice.

Melanie shrugs.

"What is it, Mel?"

"He's not supposed to go there by himself."

She sounds just like Kate, Mia thinks. She closes her eyes. Swallows hard. "Let's go find him."

Other children crowd the tide pools now, their mothers sitting nearby. Standing at the top edge of the upper pool, Mia searches for Josh among the other children and resists the impulse to close her eyes, to put her hands over her ears, to block out the sight and sound of all these people enjoying their day as if nothing were wrong.

"Is Josh lost?" Melanie looks up, squinting against the sun.

"I'll bet he ran the other way, away from the greenheads."

There are more flies now. On the far side of the ledges and the tide pools, farther down the beach to the left, a family scatters, slapping and waving their towels.

Mia approaches a woman with a toddler sitting on a blanket near the upper tide pool. "Excuse me. Have you seen my grandson? Four years old, blond, red swimsuit, carrying a Day-Glo orange pail and a green shovel?" Dan often chides her. "Less is more, honey. Especially in an emergency." This time, Mia knows the more details she offers, the more likely someone will be able to identify Josh.

The woman shakes her head. "Haven't you asked the lifeguard?"

Mia hears "yet," between the lines. "I'm on my way now."

Still holding the antiseptic pad on her left arm and sniffling, Melanie mumbles.

"What was that, Mel?"

"Josh only goes in the water if Daddy holds him."

Mia swallows hard. She clears her throat. "Of course, sweetie. He won't go in the water by himself." Melanie looks up at her, frowning, her mouth set in a white line. "She looks like Kate," Mia thinks just as she catches sight of a bright flash moving out beyond the surf line. Josh, his blond head bobbing as he is tugged out into the surf? She closes her eyes. Opens them. Focuses on the spot. And realizes the bright head belongs to a swimmer wearing a white bathing cap that appears and disappears in the waves as she swims into the surf.

With relief and a renewed sense of urgency, Mia takes Melanie's hand. Along this beach, pitched steeply down to the water in places, the breaking waves can surprise even an adult, knock you down, drag you out before you can steady yourself.

When Mia and Melanie reach the lifeguard tower, a young man dismounts. Barefoot, wearing a sleeveless sweatshirt and a cap with "Chip" embroidered on it, he has a gold crucifix on a chain around his neck. He removes his sunglasses. Blue eyes. His look steadies Mia. "What can I do for you, ma'am?"

Mia stands in front of him facing the parking lot. He gazes at the water, glancing at her from time to time as she explains about Josh. In her own ears, her voice sounds clipped and flat. Her dry eyes burn in the glare of the sand. Is he even paying attention? At the touch of his hand on her arm, Mia opens her eyes.

"As soon as my partner gets here, I'll help you. In the meantime, go back to the tide pools. Wait for me there."

Mia nods and grips Melanie's hand. She looks back once. From the foot of lifeguard tower, Chip waves and gives them a thumbs-up. She sees the second lifeguard a short distance away, approaching the tower from the parking lot.

They are nearly halfway to the tide pools, where more than a dozen children and parents are gathered. Mia wills them to leave—it's lunchtime, isn't it?—so she can see who is left behind: A single blond-haired boy, lifting hermit crabs into his new Day-Glo orange pail with his green shovel, enjoying his game, as she had hoped he would, unaware she is looking for him, that she is panicking now that she believes he's lost.

She closes her eyes. Once again, she sees Josh struggling now as he is dragged into the surf. How long had he been gone? Twenty minutes? A half an hour? Dry-mouthed, she tries to swallow.

"Why are we stopping, Mia?"

Mia forces a smile. "Just taking a closer look. Let's keep going."

As they approach the tide pools, Chip joins them, scanning the beach and the water through his binoculars. Melanie runs on ahead. Chip gestures back toward his partner, who leans against the lifeguard tower next to the rescue boat. "Maybe we'll need to put the boat in the water." He pats her shoulder.

"Mia! Down here! Here!"

Mia spots Melanie at the edge of the lower tide pool.

As soon as Mia begins to run, Melanie points down into the tide pool. There, his pail between his knees, Josh sits in the water, leaning against a boulder, scooping up hermit crabs with his green shovel.

○ ○ ○

The late-morning breeze steals into the kitchen; a paper napkin flutters from the counter, settling over Kate's garden shoes on the doormat. Hanging from a hook beside the door, the red dress slips off its hanger to the floor. Kate picks it up and buries her face in the skirt's folds, inhaling the silk's dry gingery odor. She closes her eyes, sees again her reflection in the fitting room mirror, feels the bloom of wonder rising with each breath.

The back door slams.

"Mom! Guess what? I got lost, Mom, and Mia got scared." Josh hugs her legs and looks straight up into her face, teary-eyed. He gulps, sniffs noisily, and burrows his head against her thighs.

"Slow down, sweetie. Let's have a snack first. Then you can tell me."

"No!" Josh wails, both arms around her waist, wrapping his legs around her. He begins to choke. Sitting on the floor, Kate holds and rocks him, patting his back. She looks up at Mia, standing in the doorway, expressionless. Behind her, Melanie cradles her arm.

Kate's breathing slows. The dress hanger rattles softly against the door. Josh slumps against her, pressing his face into her shoulder. She smiles up at Mia. "Let's have some lemonade."

o o o

Holding her glass of lemonade, Mia leans against the wall next to the counter, squeezing a balled-up Kleenex in the right-hand pocket of her shorts. As she tells Kate what happened, she's aware she is creating a story, one that will figure among Josh's earliest childhood memories, a story to tell at family gatherings or perhaps when he brings home a girlfriend to meet Kate and Ellis. She can imagine how it will begin. "Remember that time Mia took us to Horseneck Beach? When I got lost?" Everyone will smile and nod. It is Josh's story. Of course, he would tell it. The girl will smile, interested, and aware of her role as a newcomer: How should she respond?

"It happened so fast, Kate. He was there. And then he wasn't."

When Mia gets to the part about the lifeguard, her voice drops, her eyes close. She holds the glass of lemonade against her check. Kate pats Josh's back and speaks down into his hair. "Josh, honey, stay here while I get you some orange juice." She hands him the juice, wraps a towel around him, and stands. "Let's put an ice pack on that bite, Melanie. Why don't you take your glass out on the deck, Mia? I'll bring the lemonade out."

Kate sets the tray on the side table between the two wicker armchairs. The Waterford pitcher, a wedding gift from Mia and her father, catches the afternoon sun, casting flickering rainbows onto the deck. As she brushes the leaves from her chair, she glances at Mia sitting across from her, now holding her glass in both hands, eyes downcast, shoulders hunched. The memory of Polly's tantrum, of Mia gripping the edge of the bathtub, slides into the present, Mia, uncertain then as she is now. And afraid then—of them and their reaction to her as they stood there, together, affirming and defending their bond.

Looking out over the garden, Kate begins, "At the supermarket the other day, Josh got impatient, so I let him get down from the cart." Melanie had been helping her find grocery items, reading the labels as she went along, which slowed them down. "She couldn't find the marinara sauce." Kate laughs. "Too many choices. I found the one I wanted, and when I turned around, Josh had disappeared."

She had retraced her steps through the store. "It was just before lunch. The place was jammed." She shakes her head. "I left the cart by the ice cream freezer and took Melanie's hand. She stayed calm at first. But they hear so much about being careful in crowded places, watching out for strangers, and so forth. She started to cry." Kate sips her lemonade. "It was as if Josh had vanished. Then we got to the cookie aisle and I remembered Josh had asked me to get Animal Crackers."

Polly, Melanie, and Josh stand just inside the screen door, listening. Kate grins at them. "Josh saw us standing there at the end of the aisle and waved," she tells Mia. "He had found the Animal Crackers himself."

Followed by Melanie and Polly, Josh comes out onto the deck, carrying a plate of Animal Crackers in both hands. He offers it to Mia, then to Kate and Polly, sets the plate on the table between Kate and Mia, and helps himself.

Fairy Lights

Two months after he retired in 1984, Tom Bridgeman died of a heart attack. The day of his funeral, standing at the grave with their daughters, Julie and Darla, Vera Bridgeman gazed out over the tombstones into the woods beyond the cemetery, oblivious to the words of Tom's colleague and best friend, Jack Gardner. He spoke of Tom's gentle soul, his quiet sense of humor, his impeccable scholarship. When Julie reached for Vera's hand, she pulled away, adjusting the brim of her hat.

Darla took Julie's arm. Each carrying a bouquet of forget-me-nots, they walked to the grave's edge. As if it were her right as the elder sister, Julie dropped hers first, watching it fall on the middle of the casket lid, where it bounced once then lay crosswise, off center, leaving a space for Darla's bouquet, which landed next to it. Side by side, the two clusters of green and blue formed an incomplete ellipsis—two points awaiting the third. Julie looked back at her mother, who stood empty-handed, staring her own bouquet on the ground in front of her. Julie retrieved the flowers, took her arm, and led her gently to the grave. She looked at Julie, shook her head, and retreated.

Using the trowel in the bucket next to the grave, Julie and Darla took turns scattering soil over the casket. Behind them, their mother stood, eyes fixed on the distant trees.

Linking arms around her, Darla and Julie guided their mother back to Julie's car.

She sank into the back seat, head against the head rest. "Take me home, Julie." In the front passenger seat, Darla shook her head at Julie, who started the car. "We're going to the reception first, Mom, remember?"

Tom's colleagues had organized the reception at the faculty club. Several of them spoke, recounting anecdotes from their time at the college with Tom, some eliciting laughter. Later, their mother stood between Julie and Darla in an alcove just off the entry, acknowledging condolences with a nod and a shrug, eyes and chin lowered, shoulders hunched. Julie and Darla smiled, occasionally pressing her arm.

On the way home, Julie slowed briefly as they passed through the college gate to Main Street. "Just imagine how many times Dad drove this way."

"Should be easy to figure out," Darla said. "His schedule never changed, did it, Mom?"

Julie looked in the rearview mirror at her mother, who straightened up and leaned forward, bracing herself against the front seat. "I've got a routine too, you know. And the house and the pension," she said. "Get on with your own lives, you two. I'll be fine."

Julie glanced at Darla, who reached around and patted her mother's hand. "We'll all be fine, Mom."

Pleading fatigue and a headache, their mother went up to her room and closed the door. She'd see them in the morning, she said.

"It's weird, don't you think?" Julie set a glass of water down for Darla at her usual place across the kitchen table. For dinner, they had shared leftover roast chicken and finished the apple pie their mother had baked for the reception.

"What is?"

"She won't talk about Dad. I have no idea how she feels. Do you?"

"She has never talked about her feelings, Julie. Or anyone else's." Darla smoothed the place mat and folded her hands in front of her. "One of my patients lost her husband after a long illness. Although she talked about him often before he died, once he was gone, she never mentioned him again. It was as if he had never existed." She put down her fork and pushed her plate away.

"What did she talk about?"

"Mostly about herself, her plans. About her new life." Darla leaned back in her chair, hands in her lap.

"But Mom and Dad were married for 40 years."

Darla laughed. "Come on, Julie. You know Mom. What counts is her side of the story. Not Dad's. I'm not sure she tried to understand who he was or what he did." She folded her arms on the table. "Anyway, Julie, he's gone."

Julie remembered the sound of her father's voice, its vibration in his chest under her ear when he hugged her close, his lopsided smile, his habit of laughing at his own jokes, but these were just details, bits and pieces. This, she realized, was how it would be from now on—bits and pieces, fragments of her past and his.

The photographs of him had as little substance as a shadow that comes and goes on a cloudy day. The black-and-white portraits, formal poses, showed the world who he was in his professional life. The candid shots—birthday parties, Christmas mornings, vacations paddling their canoe on Lake Winnipesaukee—had faded and blurred, rendering him unrecognizable to all but Julie, Darla, and their mother.

She remembered him preparing his classes late into the night in his study, where she often fell asleep, observing him from the couch after she had finished her homework. She and Darla had laughed at his accounts of faculty meetings, playing the roles of different people, joking about Professors Blowhard and Full-of-herself, who managed always to derail decisions. He had also served on the board of the ASPCA for years, although their mother had forbidden him to bring home a dog or cat, claiming she was allergic. (He did what he could to make it up to them: He always took Julie and Darla with him to the local shelter when he did his volunteer time.)

"Julie?"

"I'm listening."

"I was saying that some people get depressed and spend months in treatment after the death of a spouse. Can you imagine Mom talking to me—or any other shrink, for that matter?" Darla smiled. "She's right. It's better if we just get on with our lives and leave her to hers."

"What about Dad? Our memories of Dad, I mean."

"You have yours. I have mine."

Julie imagined Darla using this tone with her patients—calm, quiet, unsparing. Her "tough love" approach.

"You don't want to talk about Dad?"

"We've just said goodbye—that's what a funeral is for. Brooding on the past or revisiting it won't change that." She pushed her hair back from her face. "My patients keep journals to record their moods, their fears, their dreams. Even if they don't write anything, I tell them to turn the page, write the date, and under the date, write 'I turned the page.' Time moves on. So can they." Darla laughed softly. "Some of them do."

"So, I should forget Dad? Move on?"

"Try keeping a journal. For a while, at least. You'll see. If you keep it up long enough, you'll find you're writing less and less about Dad; more and more about yourself. That's what death does, Julie."

"What's that?"

"It makes you face yourself."

Once, their mother had told Julie that if Darla had to hold someone's head under water to teach her to swim, she would. Her lips narrowed in a tight smile, "Darla will do whatever it takes to get the job done."

They never talked about the past, or their parents for that matter. Now, Julie realized, they would never speak about their father's death, or about how, when she got the call about his heart attack, she had collapsed, waking hours later curled up on the floor in her Boston apartment, the phone off the hook beside her, buzzing in her ear.

She wouldn't ask her mother about her feelings. That didn't keep her from wondering if—or how—her mother missed her father. What would it be like for her to live here without him, with memories linked to memories, like the paper chains she and Darla had made each year for their Christmas tree?

o o o

Visiting her mother one weekend in July, three months after the funeral, Julie helped her fold the laundry that had dried on the clothesline. "I remember this smell. Sun and the sea air. Just like the old days, don't you think?"

Her mother sniffed. "Some of them, anyway."

"The roses look better than ever this year, Mom."

"That's because I sprayed before the Japanese beetles hatched. Of course, you have to keep changing the chemicals you use." Her triumphant smile dimmed. "The beetles adapt, become immune, you know." She looked around—at the lawn, overgrown and patchy from neglect, at the flagstone patio with its round, rusting cast-iron table and chairs. "What were we talking about?"

"The beetles and the sprays? Something about changing what you use because they adapt."

"That's it, that's right."

"Is something wrong, Mom?"

"Of course not. Didn't you hear what I said about the hollyhocks? The blight?"

The hollyhocks? The blight? She had removed the hollyhocks years ago. "You mean the roses?"

"I know what I mean, Julie. I said hollyhocks. I meant hollyhocks.

Maybe you should have your hearing tested." She snatched a towel from the line, shook it hard, and folded it. "Then there's the book club, the Art Association. I'm never bored."

She held up her right hand, fist clenched, thumb stuck out. "First, there was your father." Thumb and index finger. "Then you and your father." Thumb, index, and third fingers. "Then you, Darla, and your father. All those studies about the problems people have after someone dies? People lie. Wives, especially. Truth is, it's a joy not to have to wait on anyone anymore. Enough is enough." She threw her hands up in the air. "I am just fine, thank you."

"So you don't go out with anyone?"

"With Babs, for lunch or something, once in a while." She had met Babs at a parent-teacher meeting when Julie was in the first grade.

"What about your friends from the college?"

"Those people? They're your father's friends, that crew. Not mine."

Those people? Julie couldn't remember a time when her parents hadn't given or attended a weekend dinner party, always with the same group of professors from the college where her father had taught English. *They're your father's friends.* It was as if her father's death, like a circuit breaker, had severed the connection between her mother and the community to which both had belonged.

"I thought you enjoyed those gatherings, the dinners, anyway."

"A charade." Her mouth tightened. "I went through the motions for your father's sake, to smooth the way with all of them, the ones who passed judgment when he came up for promotion." She hunched her shoulders, rubbed the back of her neck. "I learned how to cook all the fancy French dishes, sat through those pretentious avant-garde movies, and kept quiet when the others gossiped. He counted on that, your father. I even read his interminable articles—edited them, too, sometimes." She handed Julie the container of clothespins, picked up the laundry basket, and headed toward the house. At the steps, she paused, leaning forward to open the back door. "That's all in the past, Julie." She slid the basket onto the mat just inside the kitchen. "Dead and buried, like your father."

o o o

Her parents' daily life had been organized around her father's schedule—the days he taught or lectured, the days he worked at home, preparing for class or a meeting, or reading essays—her mother's chores (as she called them), her own and Darla's school work, and after-school activities. Apart from the roles they played, actors on their own domestic stage, she hadn't known them, Julie realized now. And she had never wondered what lay beneath that placid, immutable surface, or what accommodations they had reached, each to the other, to get along day after day.

Absorbed in her mother's revelation, what it meant, how it recast her assumptions about the past, Julie questioned how her mother felt deep down about being free, as she had put it. She wondered how her own and Darla's relationship with her would change. They no longer lived close by. Darla had an apartment in New York City in the same building that housed her practice. Julie had recently bought a condominium in Boston's Back Bay, not far from the bank branch she managed.

They both phoned her every week. Julie visited once a month. This pattern suited them all. None of them talked about the future. Their conversations about the present were limited to the weather, their health (always "good"), the cooking shows she watched, and her garden. Julie and Darla were getting on with their lives, just as she had directed. She never asked personal questions. (She once told Julie, "I don't care what you're thinking or how you're feeling. Just tell me what you're doing.")

One weekend in October, Julie took with her information about several cultural events in Boston. Would her mother enjoy a chamber music concert? The Impressionist exhibition at the Museum of Fine Arts? The new production of "Once Upon This Island"?

Her parents had occasionally attended performances in Boston: Her father enjoyed classical music, especially chamber music. But Julie couldn't recall her mother's reaction to these outings.

"A weekend in Boston? For one concert?" Her mother dropped the program brochure on the table with a sniff.

"You make it sound like a trip to the dentist." Julie smiled.

"Classical music." She rolled her eyes. "That was your father's thing. It's too expensive, anyway."

"And the Impressionist show?"

"So many people. You can't see the paintings, anyway. I prefer real gardens, Julie, plants you can touch and smell."

When Julie told Darla about the conversation, about her own disappointment at not being able to find something—anything— their mother might enjoy doing with her, Darla said, "She wants to be alone, Julie. That's her idea of being free, so let's not argue. She needs time to adjust to life without Dad, something she can do on her own. Let her find her own way."

"I'm worried she's spending too much time alone. And she seems confused at times."

"Occasional confusion in people Mom's age isn't unusual, really. And we can't make her see people if she doesn't want to. Look, Julie, worrying about what might happen is pointless. 'The future's not ours to see.' Remember? Dad used to sing that song."

o o o

When Julie pressed her about the occasional mishaps she reported during their phone conversations, and the ones Julie discovered when she visited—her misplaced wallet, her sprained ankle, her somewhat elevated blood pressure—her mother brushed off Julie's concern.

"There's nothing wrong with me, Julie. Even Babs is forgetful. And lots of people your age—people in their thirties—have high blood pressure. Imagine that. They've got something to worry about. Not me."

Scheduled before Tom died, then postponed five months, their mother's cataract surgeries in November were a success. Julie took time off to be with her for both. After the second one, she exulted, "I can see better now without glasses than I used to with them. I can even use eyeliner again." She batted her eyelashes and patted her hair, shorter now, and dark blond, a color that seemed to brighten her skin.

"She looks younger, Darla, not so tired and drawn."

"And coming into her own, it seems. She has a right to be happy for a change."

o o o

When Darla called for their next weekly catch-up, Julie stretched out on her couch and closed her eyes, prepared for the usual—gossip about Darla's upstairs neighbor (a womanizer), problems with her super (whose idea of an emergency was a three-alarm fire), her patients (her "problem children") who refused to follow her advice or find another shrink.

"Babs took Mom out to lunch at the Beach Inn the other day," Darla said. "She called me."

"Mom called you?"

"Sorry. I meant Babs."

Julie sat up. "That was nice of Babs. Did Mom enjoy it?"

"The server—someone new, a teenager, apparently—spilled some of Mom's iced tea on the table as she set the glass down. Mom pitched a fit, ranting about how she and Dad had been coming to the place for years, how he was probably rolling over in his grave at the sloppy service."

Julie imagined the scene, heard her mother's voice, felt her own rising panic. This had long been their mother's way with them, daily carping about grievances, real or imagined. But she was invariably—strictly—polite with service staff and had made sure Julie and Darla knew the rules: No first names; no casual conversation. Thanks delivered with eye contact.

"Babs was more upset than the server, I think."

"Why?"

"She says Mom occasionally flies into a tizzy over small annoyances. When she's out with Babs, I mean. Worse than the way she was with us at home, I gather."

"What do you think, Darla?"

"I told Babs to call if the outbursts increase in frequency, say, or if she becomes disoriented."

"What do you mean, 'disoriented'? I'd like to know more about what to look for. For when I'm down there with her myself."

"She could get lost. She could forget her name. She could become obsessed with looking for something she thinks she has lost, obsessed to the point of violent behavior—throwing things, striking out at people trying to help her, that sort of thing. She could wander off in the middle of the night in her nightgown." Darla cleared her throat and sighed. "We can't keep tabs on her all the time, Julie. And we can't prevent snits like the one in the restaurant. If she'd snapped at one of us at home we'd have ignored her like we used to, remember? This is just the way she is."

Julie imagined their mother wandering down to the harbor, to the Causeway to Goat Island, falling into the water, drowning. "I wish you were closer by."

"Babs will let us know. In an emergency, my service can reach me if I'm in session. You can reach me, too."

At least Babs lived nearby. Julie waited for Darla to point this out.

"What will be, will be, Julie. Worrying won't help."

o o o

In February, three months after the lunch with Babs, what had been episodic lapses became routine: unpaid bills; her mother's checkbook lost; her down jacket wadded up, a sodden mass in the washing machine. Julie arranged to go to Newport every weekend to straighten, clean, and shop. She persuaded her mother to hire a cleaning woman, who agreed to come three times a week for a couple of hours, an arrangement that lasted two weeks.

"She was snooping, so I fired her." Her mother shoved her hands into her pockets. "It was a terrible idea anyway." She scowled. "How many times do I have to tell you? Mind your own business. It's my life."

Standing on the front porch, her key in the lock, Julie visualized what she'd find inside—the heap of mail, newspapers, and magazines under the mail drop; the bags of groceries scattered across the hallway between the front door and the kitchen. This time, she would start with the kitchen.

The downstairs curtains were drawn, the thermostat set at 75. The air reeked of spoiling food and soiled clothing. Julie set her overnight bag down beside the door and pushed the mail into the corner. The kitchen sink and counters overflowed with pots, pans, and dishes. Dried out sandwiches, half-empty coffee mugs, and open cartons of sour milk filled the counters and table.

At first, Julie wondered how her mother could use so many dishes and utensils in one week. Now she knew. She had observed her remove a can of soup from the cupboard, place a pot on the stove, and open the can. Instead of pouring the soup into the pot, she had taken out another pot, then another can of soup, only to abandon both pots and cans. Next, she opened the bread box, removed a loaf of bread, got some sliced ham from the refrigerator, made a sandwich, placed it on a plate on the table. She then returned to the counter and made another sandwich.

"Why don't you get a tablecloth and some napkins?" Julie had suggested. "I'll finish making lunch."

Her mother went into the dining room. The drawers and doors of the credenza opened and closed several times. When she returned to the kitchen, she carried a stack of linen tablecloths and napkins, which she placed on the table. She sat and waited while Julie served their lunch, then sat across the table from her without comment.

After lunch, after she had put away the linens, Julie found a pad of paper and a pencil.

"What are you doing now, Julie?" Her mother demanded.

"Just making a shopping list, Mom. Anything special you'd like me to pick up?"

"Look in the cupboard, for Pete's sake." She flung open the cupboard door. "See for yourself," she said. "There's soup, pasta, rice, vegetables. I can get by just fine." She grabbed Julie by the wrist. "All you've ever wanted to do is spend my money." She turned away, pulling at her sweater, shaking her head, muttering, "It's my money."

Alone in the kitchen, Julie checked the cupboard: one can of tomato soup, one nearly empty box of macaroni, one can of peas. She called Darla.

o o o

Babs took their mother to her appointment for a checkup and a consultation with a psychologist. Julie came down to Newport for the follow-up.

"How did you like the doctor, Mom?"

Her mother waved her hand. "Oh, you know. These young doctors. They think they're so smart. I bet she's younger than you, Julie. What does she know, anyway?"

"Did she give you some ideas about what you can do to help yourself remember things?"

She laughed. "'Remember things'? My memory is just fine, thank you very much. I have a calendar. I mark appointment dates and that sort of thing as a reminder." She scoffed. "I'm not the one who has trouble 'remembering things.' You're the one, Julie. You've always been so forgetful. Or have you forgotten?" She laughed again, this time with genuine amusement. "Anyway, everyone is forgetful once in a while. This isn't a big deal."

"What about the bills and checks you've lost, Mom?"

"That's ridiculous. I get so much junk mail now, things are bound to get mixed up. I always find those things. They're not 'lost,' Julie. They're 'mislaid.'"

Julie called Darla as soon as they returned from the appointment while their mother was resting. "She has vascular dementia, Darla. And her blood pressure is off the charts. I'll pick up the prescription for her later."

"How did she react?"

"Of course she denied it. As she told me in the car, she's 'forgetful' once in a while, just like everyone else. To her, each event is an isolated incident. She doesn't remember how frequently she forgets, of course. When I tried to get her to talk about that, she told me I was just being picky. And 'annoying, as usual,' as she put it."

"We'll have to make sure she takes her pills. The drug will help her, so we can make plans."

"That's why the doctor suggested a daily home health aide visit. She also talked to Mom about assisted living, which, of course, she refuses even to consider. How will we persuade her, Darla?"

"I know a couple of places in Connecticut. They look just like hotels. Good ones, I mean. We might be able to talk her into taking a trip with us to visit one of them. Without telling her it's an assisted living facility, of course."

"That's the easy part. What will we do when she finds out we've tricked her?"

"Maybe she won't. Maybe when the time comes, she'll accept

what we're doing because she won't remember anything at all."

"At the end of the appointment, the doctor told her she was in pretty good shape for a seventy-five-year old."

Darla laughed. "What did Mom say to that?"

"She agreed, of course."

o o o

After a month, their mother became accustomed to the health aide's daily arrivals and departures and accepted her assistance. "No dishes, cooking, or cleaning, I told her. I can do all that myself. Besides, Julie, you can help on the weekends when you come down." Julie resumed her schedule of biweekly visits, arriving Friday evening in time to help prepare dinner, departing on the 4:00 p.m. bus to Boston on Sunday afternoon.

"She's calmer, Darla. Her blood pressure is lower. She asked me to help her order spring bulbs, remembered where she had put her list, and which form she had already filled out."

Early one Saturday morning, Julie tiptoed past her mother's room and down the stairs to sift through the week's mail on the floor beside the front door. Stuck in among the flyers, catalogs, and magazines were the bank statement and the bills her mother claimed hadn't arrived.

Absorbed in the task, Julie didn't hear her mother come downstairs and into the living room until she was there, behind her, standing so close Julie could hear her breathing. "What do you think you're doing?"

"Sorting the mail, Mom. Look. I found the bills and your bank statement."

"Stop messing with my things, you hear? I have a right to my privacy. There are laws, you know." She yanked them out of Julie's hand. Eyes narrowed and flat, she grabbed and shook Julie's ponytail. "I want you to leave. Now."

Julie struggled to stand. Her right foot had fallen asleep. "Sure, Mom. Let's have breakfast first."

As Julie reached out to take her arm, in one darting motion, her mother lifted the porcelain lamp from the hall table and threw it against the wall. The glass shade shattered. Limp in Julie's arms, breathing hard, she looked down at the shards scattered across the floor. "What happened, Julie? Who broke the lampshade, dear?"

Julie took in the pile of mail at her feet, the broken glass, the fear and confusion in her mother's eyes. "You know me, Mom, clumsy me. I'm so sorry." Holding her mother's arm, Julie led her toward the kitchen. "Why don't you fix us some tea and toast while I clean up?"

The next evening, at home in Boston, Julie called Darla. "The change happened so fast, Darla."

"At least she didn't throw it at you," Darla said.

"She could do something like that, couldn't she? We need to find her a place where she can't hurt herself or someone else. I'll start sorting and packing next weekend."

"What if she walks in on you again?"

"She's sleeping better at night. She also takes naps. I'll manage."

"I'll call the two assisted living places tomorrow, the ones that have openings."

o o o

Two weeks later, early Saturday morning, Julie crept downstairs with a roll of trash bags. In the living room, she sat on the floor and sorted the mail. She cleared the hall and living room closets and shelves, then moved on to the utility cabinet and kitchen cupboards. By 8 o'clock when her mother got up, she had finished the downstairs. The heap of trash bags she placed in the driveway dwarfed the garbage bins.

Darla called just after ten. "How's it going?"

Julie rubbed out a fingerprint on the wall next to the phone. "I'm winning, I guess. She seems okay this morning, but she hasn't noticed the boxes I stacked in the living room."

Their mother had been a finicky housekeeper and a stickler for details, like how to iron the button-down collars on their blouses. She had taught them her spray starch technique, had them practice on dishtowels until they had perfected it. And she wouldn't allow them buy white leather shoes: Too hard to clean, impossible to polish away the scuff marks.

"Have you found anything important?"

"'Important' like stock certificates, or hundred-dollar bills, you mean?"

Darla laughed. "Or love letters?"

"Not even close," Julie scoffed. "Nothing but odds and ends. Duplicate this; triplicate that. Just stuff." It felt like a betrayal, revealing to Darla how far their mother had slipped. "Dried out tubes of toothpaste; thirty used-up lipsticks; a batch of mascaras; nail polish; string; Scotch tape; shopping lists; receipts; hair pins. And the diamond earring she lost fifteen years ago."

"I'd keep that, at least," Darla said. "And don't tell her you found it, Julie. It will only upset her. It's unlikely she remembers she lost it. Bag and toss everything else."

"I also found more unpaid bills, which I'll pay, of course."

"Will you finish today?"

"By the time I leave tomorrow, anyway. Fortunately, Monday is trash day."

A hoarder had lived in Julie's building in Boston. Fifty years of magazines and newspapers stacked to the ceiling allowed a path barely a foot wide for him to pass from one room to another in his three-room apartment. He had suffocated when the stacks in the living room collapsed on top of him. Nearly a month went by before a neighbor realized something was wrong.

Imagine being buried under hundreds of pounds of magazines and newspapers, their yellowing pages to dust, the events and the lives and loves of those involved long forgotten.

What about their mother's brain, its synapses failing, her mind emptying of memories once vibrant and filled with meaning? Each bag Julie tied and placed in the driveway, each box she taped and stacked in the living room, held a miscellany of relics, their history long forgotten. "I still think about all those slivers of hand soap she saved and stored in jars. What for?"

"And the tinfoil, used and reused, so worn out flakes of it turned up in the soup?" Darla chuckled.

"And all those stories about making do in the Depression. Remember how she always told us, 'Waste not, want not'? To her, this made sense. But rubber bands to hold up my socks when the elastic at the top wore out? The Depression was over. I didn't want anyone to know how poor we were."

"You mean, how poor Mom thought we were," Darla interjected.

"I was so embarrassed." Julie had wanted to help, to cooperate in any way she could. Still, at school she removed the rubber bands from her socks. What did it matter that the tops flopped down over her shoes? Who, besides their mother, even noticed?

"Remember how she used clear nail polish to stop the runs in our stockings so she wouldn't have to buy us new ones?"

"And turned the collars on our blouses to make them last longer." The coupons and Green Stamps, the taking in and letting out of skirts and dresses, the shortening or lengthening of hems were her badge of honor.

o o o

Separated from the kitchen by a narrow hallway, their father's study had floor-to-ceiling bookshelves to the left and the right of the door.

Opposite the door, above the desk, a plate-glass window overlooked the back lawn and border garden, and a sycamore maple, a bed of pachysandra planted around the base. From mid-June until late September, the tree cast dappled shade over the lawn and border. Their mother had made peace with it after attempting to grow the roses she preferred. Instead, she had planted different varieties of hosta, ferns, coleus, and hydrangeas, all of which thrived in its shadow. On the southwest, treeless side of the house, where they and the laundry benefited from the sun exposure, she had planted the hybrid tea roses transplanted from her garden in Princeton, and her pride and joy, the French climbing rose, Madame Alfred Carrière. It wound its way through and up the trellis Tom had attached to the house.

Julie stood in the open door taking in her father's desk, his chair, the green-shaded brass lamp he'd had since she was a child. How many hours had he spent in that chair, a student paper before him on the blotter, a pencil in his left hand, jotting notes? Often, she had come in from school to sit on the floor, reading while he worked.

His pipe, lying on the tray of paper clips, pens, and pencils, smelled strongly of his favorite Dunhill tobacco. His tweed jacket, worn thin at the elbows, which her mother had patched and re-patched for years, hung on the brass hook on the back of the door. Julie took it off the hook and wrapped it around her shoulders and inhaled: Old Spice and Dunhill, Scottish Blend.

A cassette player sat next to the typewriter on the shelf of the fold-out typing stand. Julie pushed "play." The opening bars of Schubert's "Death and the Maiden" swept into the room. Her father had taken her to hear the Guarneri perform in Boston. She had worn a blue taffeta dress with a white organdy collar; patent leather Mary Janes; and a camelhair coat. A tall blonde woman had nodded at her father and smiled at Julie. When Julie asked him who she was, he'd shrugged. "Another Schubert fan." Then he winked and smiled. "Someone else who thinks you look very nice in that dress."

It was as if he were standing there, next to her now.

Julie sat in the desk chair and opened the top right-hand drawer. Filled with neatly labelled folders, it held correspondence and department meeting bulletins. One at a time, before discarding them, Julie flipped through them. Her father had attached copies of his replies to letters he had received. It appeared he had kept every department meeting bulletin dating back to the beginning of his career. Had he intended to do something with them? Write about his experiences as a faculty member, perhaps?

In the second drawer were his lecture notes arranged by course title—The Romantics; Shakespeare: The Tragedies; Essay Writing. Once he had mentioned giving a paper about teaching Shakespeare's tragedies to students whose lives had been touched by the Kennedy and King assassinations, the Civil Rights movement and Vietnam. Hamlet, Prince of Denmark? Maybe thinking about the death of a revered President could help them enter the world of tragic events dramatized in these plays, tragic events that otherwise seemed foreign to them, expressed in a language they struggled to understand. Or had they become so inured to the horror of brutal, sudden death, Shakespeare's tragedies were too stilted, too formal, too theatrical to elicit any feeling at all? Disappointed not to find the paper, or even his notes for it, Julie dumped everything into the trash bag.

He had published *Jane Austen's World*, still a standard reference among Austen scholars. It had been his one contribution to the field. Articles and conference talks followed, but over the years he lost interest in the wider academic world. His passion for teaching had faded, too. Grumbling that his students seemed incapable of writing simple declarative sentences, he spent less and less time at the college.

He'd been an amateur birdwatcher. Instead of preparing new courses, he took his binoculars and a picnic lunch and paddled his canoe into the nearby inlets and marshes, becoming a volunteer spotter for the Christmas Bird Count every year. When she didn't have homework or house chores, Julie went along on these excursions, spending hours on the water learning by her father's example how to observe the birds, noting each by name, place, and date in the spiral notebook he had given her.

Nothing in the file drawer attested to this interest. Anyone who didn't know about his interest in birding might have concluded that he divided his time equally between teaching his classes or attending meetings at the college and preparing his courses or grading the student papers and exams at home. Julie wondered if his colleagues guessed he spent as much time on the water, weather permitting, as he spent performing the duties associated with his job.

When Julie tried to close the second drawer, it stuck. She jiggled it back and forth, to no avail. By jamming a wooden ruler under it, she managed to release it from the rails, emptied it, and turned it upside down: A coiled string of red, heart-shaped lights was taped to the bottom with an index card that read, "Julie."

o o o

In August 1952, three weeks after Julie's eighth birthday, two months after Tom's successful defense of his thesis, they moved from Princeton, to Newport, Rhode Island, where Tom had found a position teaching English at the local college. They had arrived at the new house on Friday night. On Saturday morning, soon after the moving van pulled up in front, as he helped the men unload, her father discovered he had left all his tools behind on the pegboard in the front hall closet of the Princeton house, a pegboard where her mother had positioned and outlined every tool in Magic Marker.

"Your mother's a real stickler, Julie," her father said when he first showed her the pegboard, the tools neatly arranged and hung on it.

"What's a stickler?"

"Someone who believes there's a right way and a wrong way and makes sure you know the difference—and follow the rules. Like here:

Mom drew the outline of each tool so I'll always put each one where it belongs." He smiled. "The same way she helps you put your books back on the shelf every day."

Upstairs in her new bedroom in her sleeping bag on the floor, her parents arguing in the kitchen below woke her the next morning.

"How could you forget?" her mother demanded.

"Does it matter? They're just tools. Replaceable tools. A wrench, a couple of screwdrivers, three plyers. Not a big deal."

"To you, nothing's a big deal. We have an eight-year-old who outgrows her clothes the minute she puts them on and a baby on the way. And a mortgage. How am I supposed to pay for a new set of tools? On the pittance they're paying you, you'll just have to borrow the screwdriver or the wrench, whatever, when you need it. Anyway, it's not like you use them every day."

"Just take Julie with you to the hardware store, buy a wrench, a screwdriver, and a hammer. That'll be all I need for now."

The kitchen door slammed. Soon the faint sweet smell of her father's pipe smoke drifted into her room from the front porch, mingling with the smell of brewing coffee. Julie squeezed her eyes shut, remembering the white house on Maple Street, its green shutters and red brick steps, the flower boxes where her mother planted petunias every spring, the dogwood tree in the middle of the front lawn. That was home.

This was still "the new house."

o o o

When her mother parked in front of the hardware store, it had just opened. Dwarfed by the stacks of lumber beside it that ran the length of the lot, the one-story building had three front entrances, with shopping carts and baskets lined up in racks. Inside, people milled around, some with baskets, some with carts, a few, empty-handed.

As soon as they entered the store, Julie realized it was much larger than it appeared from outside. Lined with floor-to-ceiling shelves crammed with supplies, the aisles stretched from the front doors to the back, narrowing in the distance just like the highway as they drove to Newport from Princeton. Julie imagined filling a cart with saws, screwdrivers, drills, wrenches, and pliers, so that her father would never have to borrow tools from anyone else. She imagined him speaking to an acquaintance, "A wrench? A screwdriver? No problem. Just tell me what you need. Happy to lend you one of mine."

"Julie! Did you hear me?

"What?"

"Wait for me over there, by that blue bin. I won't be gone long." She looked up at the signs hanging over each aisle and shook her head. "However long it takes, stay put. You hear?"

"Yes, Mom."

o o o

Julie watched her mother disappear down one of the aisles, mingling with other shoppers, some consulting lists, others wending their way through the Saturday morning crowd. Just tall enough to peer over the top of the blue bin—it came up to her shoulders—she saw that it contained odds and ends. She hiked herself up over the top to take a closer look: rolls of tape, packages of thumbtacks, hose nozzles, door hinges, tubes of Super Glue, a flyswatter shaped like a butterfly, a can opener, a dish rack, a collection of drill bits, some of them missing— most in their original packages, now torn and taped.

Tucked under the dishrack, a gleam of cellophane, the glint of something red, caught her eye.

The slick, lumpy package seemed to sink as she reached for it, un- til she managed to grasp its edge between her thumb and forefinger. Holding it tight, she pushed herself out of the bin down to the floor.

The package contained a tangled string of lights, bunched and taped to a cardboard insert. Each the size and shape of a candy heart, the bulbs were dark red, the color of her mother's nail polish.

"'Fairy Lights,' dear. Those are fairy lights." Standing behind her, a woman reached over her shoulder into the bin. Julie shrugged away from her, clasping the lights to her chest.

The woman laughed. "It's the thumbtacks I want, dear." She reached into the bin and pulled out the package. "Hang on to those fairy lights," she said, smiling. "They're a treasure, all right."

Reflecting the overhead lights, the miniature hearts seemed to glow like the taillights of the cars and trucks moving through the night on the New Jersey Turnpike the night before. Kneeling on the backseat, her chin on the seat back between the two headrests, Julie had followed the lights as they disappeared in the dark, heading south, toward Princeton and the white house with the green shutters on Maple Street, where she had lived her whole life. Until yesterday. *Home.*

o o o

On the ceiling of her room in Princeton, her father had pasted the glow-in-the-dark constellations, the Big Dipper, the Little Dipper, and Polaris. "Polaris, that's the North Star, Julie."

Every night she had fallen asleep under the faint, green glow. Long ago, her father had told her, sailors had charted their course with Polaris in sight. "Imagine figuring out how to get home with only the North Star and the horizon to guide you."

"What if it was cloudy or snowing?"

"Then they held the course they set as best they could, until they could check their position. Sometimes, if they got caught in a big storm, that took days, even weeks." He pulled her closer.

"Are you sad, Daddy?"

"Sometimes the sailors didn't make it home. Not all of them, anyway."

Julie imagined the sailors blown overboard into the cold, dark water, hearing their shipmates' panicked cries, watching the glow of the ship's lanterns recede and disappear, going home, leaving them behind alone in the dark, drowning.

He had hugged her. "You're safe, sweetheart. No storm will blow this little ship off course."

o o o

"Julie!" Wallet in one hand, coupon book in the other, her mother beckoned to her from the checkout counter.

The cashier smiled at Julie. "That too?"

Her mother frowned.

"Please, Mom? They're only a dollar. I'll pay for them myself with my allowance—next week's allowance, I mean." Julie's allowance was the change her father had left in his pocket at the end of the week. Sometimes this was as much as a dollar. Most of the time, it was less.

The man behind them in line shook his head and looked away.

"For my room? Please?" Other people farther behind them in line stared, shuffling their feet, reaching into pockets and purses for their wallets, as if that would speed things up.

Her mother gave the package of lights and a dollar bill to the clerk. The clerk handed her the bag of tools she had already paid for. He then rang up the fairy lights and handed the receipt and a small bag to Julie. "They don't make these anymore," he told her, smiling. "They are very special."

o o o

When they had arrived at the store earlier, the parking lot had been almost empty. Now it was full. Her mother frowned at the signs at the end of each row of cars. "Did I park in row 'A' or row 'B'?" She sighed and took Julie's hand. "At least it's a VW bus we're looking for, not a Beetle." She scanned the 'A' row. No VW bus there.

"Let's try 'B'." She let go of Julie's hand. "Stay right behind me, now." She walked between the parked cars until she reached the roadway, where she took Julie's hand again and waited for a car to pass.

"Oh, no." Her mother looked down: A blob of pink bubble gum stuck to the heel of her right sandal.

"There's the bus, right over there, Mom."

"Don't shout, Julie." Walking gingerly on the ball of her right foot, her mother made it to the car, opened the back door for Julie, and slid her shopping bag across the seat, motioning to Julie to get in. She opened the driver's door, sat on the driver's seat and took off the sandal, which she tossed into the well on the passenger's side. Holding her package in her lap, Julie looked up at the rearview mirror. Her mother's eyes, hot and red with tears, stared back at her.

"Why are you crying, Mommy?"

"Hush, Julie." She blew her nose and started the car.

o o o

As soon as they turned the corner, Julie recognized their new house. Unlike the others on the street, it was built of brick, a bay window facing the street. Its front steps were also brick with a white handrail, chipped and worn. Stacks of boxes and piles of crumpled paper cluttered the driveway and the front walk. While Julie and her mother had been at the hardware store, the movers had returned to finish unloading the van. One of them wheeled a cart piled high with boxes into the garage. Her father sat on the front steps, smoking his pipe. When her mother handed him the bag of tools, he looked at her bare foot and the sandal in her hand.

"What happened?"

"Bubblegum." Her mother's eyes shifted sideways. She rubbed her lower back. "Maybe alcohol will take it off."

"Go on in, Vera. I'll find something." He took the sandal from her and turned to Julie.

"What's in your bag?"

"Fairy lights. That's what the lady told me. What are fairy lights, anyway?"

Her father smiled. "The ones I know about twinkle, like Tinker Bell. And they're white." He shrugged. "I guess that's why they call them fairy lights. But these? If these are fairy lights, they're special ones. Maybe they're a signal of some kind, an invitation to fairies to come for a visit? We'll have to wait and see." His smile told her he meant it: They would wait and see together.

Sometimes, it seemed to Julie that her father could think her thoughts, that he felt her feelings. After dinner that night, he hammered three hooks into the wall above the window in her room and draped the string of lights across the top and down each side of the window frame like a necklace. "Fairy lights at night; sunrise in the morning. Aren't you the lucky one?" Each of the lights cast its own glowing halo against the window frame and wall.

Awake in the dark in her bed across from the window, gazing at the lights and their reflection, Julie wondered what fairies looked like. Were they even visible? Of course, she had seen drawings of them in books, like the ones of Tinker Bell. But weren't those drawings just the way someone imagined fairies looked? Suppose real fairies were invisible? Or too small to see without using a magnifying glass? If they came, guided by the lights, how would she know? Would they leave presents, like Santa Claus? Or money, like the Tooth Fairy?

o o o

Every night Julie waited, following the lights' path around the window and back again, until she fell asleep. Sometimes the lights seemed to flicker. Sometimes, their halos seemed to expand and contract as she breathed.

When Darla was born six months later, her mother moved the crib into Julie's room and took down the lights.

"Why, Mom? Why can't you leave the lights? Darla doesn't care. She's just a baby."

"They'll keep her awake, Julie. She needs to sleep." Her mother gave her father a look. "So do I."

"How do you know? She can't talk, she can't do anything. She's just a dumb baby."

For days, Julie felt the sting of her mother's slap. At night, she cried herself to sleep.

Sometimes, wakened by Darla's fussing, Julie closed her eyes and imagined the lights, traced their glowing path around the window, holding onto this vision until it merged with her memory of the taillights disappearing into the dark, heading south toward Princeton, toward the white house on Maple Street.

Fireflies

The screen door slams. "Hey, Liz?" Sunny calls, "I've got bread!"

Liz gets up from her desk, tiptoes across the room, and closes the door, holding her breath. Maybe Sunny will take the hint, put the bread on the kitchen counter and leave.

"I've got news, too." Sunny takes the stairs two at a time and opens the door. "You need to find a better hiding place."

"Can't it wait?" Liz waves at her worktable and the floor. "I'm slammed." Sketches, plant lists, estimates, schedules—all the elements of her garden design for the local library—lie in piles on her floor, on her desk, even on the windowsill. By the end of the afternoon, when she has assembled the presentation portfolio, she will make copies for the planning committee members. Tomorrow, they'll make their final decision about her proposal. It is a pro bono project. If they turn it down, she will bow out. She needs to get back to earning a living.

Sunny grins. "He looks good, Liz." Like a cat gauging the distance to a mouse it has cornered, she adds, "Real good."

He? Sunny has a new boyfriend? "Sounds like a dessert." Liz scoffs.

Shirt untucked, face smudged with flour, Sunny shoves her hands into her pockets and leans against the doorjamb. "Aren't you at least curious?"

Liz eyes the clock. "Just tell me, okay?"

Sunny straightens up. "Come have a cup of coffee and a slice of my latest experiment while I fill you in."

Liz looks up at the clock over her window. Twenty to three. She needs at least two hours to finish and copy the proposal in time to shower and dress for her mother's dinner party. "Twenty minutes."

Sunny pumps her fist. "You won't be sorry."

o o o

Outside the kitchen window, the crabapple branches lift their blossoms to the afternoon sun. The hay field across the road from the house ripples and tosses in the breeze, a sign that the second cutting is near. In the distance, the church's brass weathervane flashes beneath the cloudless sky, where a solitary contrail now drifts, its edges blurred.

Sunny stands at the sink filling the espresso pot, her blond hair hanging in an untidy braid down her back. She smiles at Liz over her shoulder. "It'll go great tomorrow. You'll see."

"At least they nixed the sculpture of the peeing urchin." One of the library board members had wanted to donate the sculpture and its pool, an inheritance from a British uncle. The committee chairman told him it would attract the wrong kind of attention, distracting from the new garden and its local designer. Liz shudders at the thought. No more negative publicity, please.

What did people in town think of her and Sunny now, she wondered? So much had come out after their father's death fifteen years ago. Maybe they'd tired of hearing about what had gone on for years behind closed doors. Maybe now that bipolar disorder carried less of a stigma, their horror had given way to sympathy. Besides, during his calm periods, hadn't Doc Thomson been a fine physician? At his memorial service, many had said so.

Still, surely some of them thought it strange that she and Sunny had come back, that neither had married. Sunny explained that she had travelled around the world learning how to bake. Was she planning to open her own bakery here, in Stanton (population 1250), some asked? Sunny demurred. Then, when the village's only grocery store closed, she bought and gutted it, and transformed it into Sunnyside Up. She laughed at the doubters. "I'm a baker," she said. "It's what I like to do. Lucky for me, it's what I do best." As if that were enough to assure her success.

Within a few months of being hired by a landscape design firm in Boston, Liz knew it wouldn't last. First, there was the competition among the junior staff. "Who you know matters more than what you know," she told Sunny. "It's like being in seventh grade." Then, a colleague took credit for Liz's work on a major project. Although she'd only had the job for eight months, she decided to leave. Once her boss realized she wouldn't change her mind, he promised to send referrals her way. "You won't make a living at first, but you'll make good contacts." *And I won't have to deal with office politics.*

Liz had returned to Stanton three years ago, a year after Sunny. Their mother, Judith, a realtor, had found her the farmhouse to rent on the other side of the village from the house they'd grown up in, where Judith still lived. Did people talk about that? Not that she and Sunny had come back, not that now, in their mid-thirties, both remained single and childless, but that their mother had kept the house after their father hanged himself from a rafter in the barn.

o o o

Sunny removed the loaf of bread from the basket and held it over her head like a trophy. "Gluten-free. But you'd never guess."

Her baking experiments often produced unique results. After each trial run, she made notes and adjustments, gave the loaves to friends or bagged them to feed to the ducks. Casual about everything else in her life—her unruly hair, her torn jeans, her battered clogs—

in the baking department she was attentive down to the last quarter teaspoon.

While Sunny slices the bread, Liz keeps an eye on the espresso pot, ignoring Sunny's sidelong looks.

Liz sets mugs, jam, and plates on the table and pulls up a chair. "So, tell me about 'Dessert Man.'"

"Thought you'd never ask." Sunny leans across the table and stage-whispers, "It's Jeff, Liz. He's back, with Jessie—she's his wife—and their baby. They came into the bakery this morning."

Liz watches someone else's hand spoon some strawberry jam over the bread on her plate. Someone else's hand grips the handle of the mug on the table. The mug rises to her lips. She takes a sip.

"Come on, Liz. I can tell you're dying to know." Sunny leans back. A blue-eyed blonde, she has a blonde's creamy complexion, a baker's rounded figure.

"Tell me." Liz sees him grinning at her, his T-shirt sweat-damp, his jeans low-slung. Seventeen years ago: 2004.

"Still has that rocker look, a bit ridiculous on a 34-year-old dad." Sunny rolls her eyes. "Jessie seems nice, about my age, blondish, ponytail. And the baby is adorable, of course." Sunny cuts and hands Liz another slice of bread. "Anyway, maybe you'll have a chance to see for yourself." She spreads jam on her own slice and takes a bite. "What do you think?"

"About?"

"About the bread, Liz." Another eyeroll.

Sunny had always known how to get a rise out of her. Seventeen years ago, Jeff had nicknamed Liz Enya, because she wore her dark hair in a shag, played the guitar, and sang Enya's song "I want tomorrow," in a high, sweet soprano. She was also a track star, long-legged and lean—the opposite of Sunny, who had taunted her, "You should have been a guy."

Liz can't taste anything. She focuses on the bread's texture—not gluey, the quality she associated with everything gluten-free. "Gluten-free, really?"

"My third tweak." Sunny picks up the cut loaf, sniffs it. She puts it down. Glances at Liz. "They'll be here a week or two, he said."

Liz begins to choke. She waves off the glass of water Sunny pushes toward her, fighting for breath, wiping away the tears with her napkin. "I don't care," she gasps.

"Of course not." Sunny drains her mug and wipes her mouth.

Liz crumples her napkin. "Did he ask about me?"

Sunny smiles. "I'm sure he's forgiven you."

o o o

In November of 2004, their junior year, Liz and her best friend, Alison, both waiting for the late bus, had been talking about the homecoming dance.

"Is Sunny coming with you and Jeff?"

"Maybe," Liz replied. "Why?"

"Seems like she and Jeff have been spending a lot of time together."

"So?" Liz set her books down on the bench next to the bike rack near the waiting area.

"Kids are talking."

"About what? Sunny doesn't like to walk home in the dark. So Jeff gives her a ride sometimes, like when I stay late for track. And she's crazy about that car." Jeff had a powder-blue Impala he called "The Blue Goose." He had restored it himself. "Come on, Ali, what's going on?"

"Promise not to get mad at me?"

"Of course, I won't get mad at you."

"Tom says Sunny sits so close, it's like she's sitting in Jeff's lap."

On the way home in the bus, Liz shut her eyes, imagining the scene. She sat that close to Jeff sometimes, his arm around her shoulder, his hand close to, but not touching, her right breast.

First she confronted Sunny, who cried and blamed Jeff.

The next day, Liz cornered Jeff in the cafeteria. "Sunny? Really? Why would I?" he laughed.

"Just answer the question, Jeff. Does she or doesn't she sit beside you?"

He sighed. "Aw, come on, Liz. It's just flirting. That's all."

"That's not what it looks like."

"Says who?"

"Says Tom."

Jeff slipped his thumbs into the waistband of her jeans, pulled her close, kissed her. "She's only fourteen, you know."

A few days later, Liz took her mother's station wagon—to pick up a book she'd left in her locker, she told her. She found the Blue Goose parked in its usual corner spot on the side street nearest the high school. With no parking spot in front of him, Jeff told her, no driver could back into him.

When the cross traffic cleared, Liz pulled into the middle of the intersection, checked to be sure no one was watching and backed up. There was a crunch, then a clang as the Impala's front bumper hit the pavement. She checked the rearview mirror. Still no one in sight. The bumper hung there, half on, half off. Just a normal, hit-and-run fender-bender. The next day, everyone knew about the damaged Blue Goose. The cause of the damage ran a gamut: a rival football team member; a speeder taking the corner too fast; a near-sighted little old lady. Did Jeff suspect her, she wondered? She had caught him looking at her once as if maybe he did.

o o o

At 5 o'clock, the phone rings; the answering machine clicks on. "Liz, honey? Pick up, would you?"

Liz lifts the receiver. "Hi, Mom."

"You're bringing vegetables and dip?"

"And I'll be there at 7." The silence at her mother's end lengthens. "Mom?"

"There's one other thing." Her mother's tone, warm and intimate, puts Liz on guard, tells her she won't like "this one other thing," whatever it is. "I've invited Jeff, Jessie—that's his wife—and their baby."

Had Sunny known? Liz looks out the window, sees a hawk dive, wonders if the rabbit felt the way she does—trapped and helpless. "I'll be there. But I won't stay long. I've got my presentation tomorrow, remember?"

"He's a family friend, Liz. I haven't seen him since your father died. I'd like to meet his wife and baby. The business with his car? That was years ago."

"Seventeen years, Mom."

"That's what I said. A long time."

Anger and betrayal give no quarter. Seventeen years ago, the sweet taste of revenge had quickly dissipated. Her mother had confronted her. And when she learned the truth, she had paid to repair both cars, becoming Sunny and Jeff's accomplice in Liz's humiliation.

"Let it go, Liz. This dinner party is for Charles, remember."

"Mom, please, couldn't you—?"

"What's past is past, Liz."

o o o

What's past is past. The lesson their mother had tried so hard to teach them.

She had covered up each of their father's breakdowns, as though his affliction were something to be ashamed of. She didn't— couldn't?—acknowledge its seriousness. She sent Liz and Sunny to stay with a friend—the only friend who knew about his condition. She hired a service to clean up and dispose of the smashed furniture, the broken dishes and glasses, and a handyman to plaster and paint over the holes in the walls. Her father was certain that's where the forces that persecuted him were hiding

Her mother's resolve had cracked when he tried to burn the house down. That time, she had committed him to a treatment center for three months. She wrote a letter to his patients, explaining that he'd been invited to fill in for a friend who had taken a medical leave. She didn't say where he was or how long he'd be away. Sworn to secrecy, his assistant handled routine matters, such as physicals and messages, and referred urgent cases to the hospital emergency room.

Liz understood why her mother had worked so hard to conceal the truth. A successful realtor, she had her own business—and her reputation—to manage. She also wanted to protect Liz and Sunny. But over time, their father's breakdowns became more frequent, more violent. Once complicit in maintaining the pretense all was well, Liz found reasons not to come home from college, staying with friends whenever she could. The price of going home—living in constant fear of the next blowup—was too high.

When her mother had confronted her about the damage to her station wagon, Liz confessed. She had listened in on her mother's phone conversation, her apology to Jeff's father, accepting responsibility for the accident, promising to take care of it—to cover it up.

What was done was done. Liz had broken up with Jeff the next day.

When Sunny came home from summer camp and the school year began, she and Jeff kept their distance from one another. By Thanksgiving, Sunny and Liz carried on as if Sunny's flirtation with Jeff had never happened.

As she dresses for the party, Liz realizes the episode's emotional toll had only been dormant, revived now by her anxiety about seeing

Jeff again. If she can focus on Charles, the guest of honor, whom her mother had been seeing for six months, she'll be all right.

If only Jeff would do the same.

o o o

Silhouetted against the sunset, a half dozen pin oaks flank the driveway to the barn, the woods behind them already deeply shadowed. To the right of the barn and up a slight rise, with its mullioned windows and center chimney, the square, grey-shingled house stands, plain-spoken and stolid.

On the screened-in porch, her mother and Sunny light candles and arrange the furniture. Holding the platter of vegetables, Liz leans against her car, listening to their voices and laughter. Here and there in the dusk a firefly flashes, harbinger of the swarms that will soon gather, rising and falling in waves in the underbrush and over the lawn.

"That you, Liz?"

She turns toward his voice, bumping her elbow against the side mirror, jostling the platter. "Hi, Charles."

A retired lawyer, Charles Stanley is 73, two years older than her mother. His wife had died four years ago. House-hunting in the area, he had contacted Judith, who had helped him find and purchase an old house near the center of town. Tall, stoop-shouldered, silver-haired, he is at ease with himself and the world. Now he leans toward her, supporting himself on a cane. "Everything okay?"

"Fine, yes."

Right hand on his cane, left hand holding a bouquet of daisies, he bends from the waist to kiss her cheek. Liz takes his left elbow. "Shall we?"

Fireflies swirl around them and across the lawn. One lands on Liz, briefly casting its pale light on her bare shoulder. In the darkening woods behind the house, the insects form eddies above the underbrush. On the porch, candles flicker among the glass vases of roses, sunflowers, and snapdragons. Liz places her platter of vegetables on the sideboard between a tray of cheese and a basket of crackers. Her mother hugs Charles. "Did Liz tell you?"

Charles smiles at Liz. "About?"

"One of her friends from high school and his wife and their baby—a little girl, I believe—are coming too," her mother says, her eyes on Liz as she makes room for the vegetable platter next to the cheese tray.

Charles nods.

Her father would have told the story of the bumper—her "unfinished business," he'd called it. He hadn't liked Jeff, considered him "crude." At the time, her father's objections had enhanced Jeff's appeal—until she found out about his drives with Sunny.

Voices and laughter and the sound of a stroller's wheels on the gravel path announce the arrival of Jeff, Jessie, and the baby. Charles hands Liz a glass of wine and stands beside her.

∘ ∘ ∘

Carrying the baby, Jessie pushes the stroller through the screen door followed by Jeff, a canvas carry-all over his shoulder, which he sets down on the floor against the wall beside an end table. In candlelight, he looks the same—his right eyebrow higher than the left, his hair, shorter now, its waves still combed and placed just so. Liz had sketched his portrait so often, eventually she could do it from memory. Did he still have the charcoal version, the one she gave him for his sixteenth birthday?

Before she says anything he's there, pulling her to him. She closes her eyes. The flutter of his breath, the pressure and shape of his lips on her cheek, bring back the fragrance of the leather conditioner he'd used on the Impala's upholstery, the clicks of its engine as it cooled in the dark spring night. She feels again his arm around her shoulder, his thumb touching the edge of her sleeveless blouse.

As her mother introduces Charles and Jeff, Jessie introduces herself to Liz. Now in her stroller, the baby begins to fuss. "Sweet thing," Jessie rocks the stroller gently. "Remember our deal? You're supposed to sleep through drinks." Eyes wide, the baby looks up at her, smiles.

Jessie lifts her from the stroller. "Liz, meet Lizzie."

Liz touches the baby's cheek. "Hello, Lizzie."

Lizzie gurgles. Liz and Jessie laugh.

"She's named after my grandmother, Elizabeth. We called her Lizzie," Jessie explains. She nuzzles the baby's head. "I didn't find out about you and Jeff until after."

How much does Jessie know, Liz wonders? Probably Jeff stressed how put out he was about the car. Maybe the story amused her, how two sisters' competition for the same boyfriend led to a car crash? Had he told her that they'd broken up, that her mother had paid to repair his car, that she, Liz, had called ahead before every party that summer to make sure Jeff hadn't been invited. Only once had he shown up unexpectedly. As soon as he spotted her, he left. Liz glances at him across the porch. He doesn't notice.

Jessie rocks Lizzie from side to side. "She needs a change. Could I do it in the house?"

"There's a window seat in the living room, just inside the door."

"Could you hold her while I get her blanket and the bag?"

Liz feels Jeff's eyes following them as she, Jessie, and Lizzie cross the porch into the living room.

o o o

Jessie smooths the changing blanket on the window seat and lays the baby on it. Liz sits cross-legged on the floor, leaning against an armchair. Blond and voluptuous like Sunny, Jessie has square, capable-looking hands, like Sunny's. Just like Sunny, who can manipulate delicate pastry crust into its baking pan without tearing it, Jessie manages to remove and replace Lizzie's diaper without distressing her. She's younger than Sunny, Liz realizes, probably in her mid-twenties.

Jessie looks up, catching her by surprise. "Are you okay?"

Liz forces a smile. "Just wondering if you need anything? Washcloth? Towel?"

"As long as she doesn't start kicking, all I need is speed." Jessie laughs. "Done." She pats Lizzie's tummy and lifts her so that she looks toward the door to the porch over Jessie's shoulder. Wide awake, Lizzie coos and giggles. Liz turns, expecting to see Jeff. But it's Sunny who stands in the doorway a cracker in one hand, a carrot stick in the other. "That's what I call a warm welcome," she says. Lizzie reaches toward her, gurgling.

Sunny pops the cracker into her mouth and puts the carrot stick on the side table. "May I?" she asks. Jessie hands her the baby. Settled in Sunny's arms, Lizzie crows. "Let's get a drink, shall we?" Sunny says, nodding in the direction of the porch.

Carrying Lizzie, Sunny leads them back to the porch. Side by side on one of the wicker settees, Charles and Jeff face her mother, sitting on the settee across from them. Their wine glasses, cocktail napkins, a bottle of white wine, and Liz's vegetable platter take up most of the coffee table between them. They're discussing local politics.

"Such a treat to gossip with someone who's been away," her mother says, holding out her hand to Jeff.

With Lizzie on her lap, Sunny sits on the settee beside her mother. Jessie carries a wicker chair from the corner of the porch and joins them. Lizzie plays with Sunny's beads, while Sunny answers Jessie's questions about the bakery. Jeff, talking to Judith, watches Liz, sitting on a chair next to Charles, talking to him about some changes he has in mind for his garden.

During a lull in the conversation, her mother catches Liz's eye, lifts her chin, and eyes the kitchen.

Is her mother trying to spare her the awkwardness of making conversation with Jessie and Jeff? So far, Liz thinks, she deserves credit for good behavior. Awkward as it was, Jeff's kiss was just a kiss, after all. Didn't that show she's doing her part to make sure that what's past stays in the past?

"What's so funny?" Sunny asks.

Liz shakes her head. "Later."

o o o

Leaves of Boston lettuce soak in cold water in the sink. Tomato soup, fragrant with basil, simmers on the stove. Slipping her mother's apron over her head and tying it around her waist, Liz gazes at her reflection in the window above the sink. Pale, the furrow between her eyebrows a dark shadow, she looks as tired as she feels. She should have stayed home, reviewed her presentation one last time before tomorrow's meeting, which was likely to be as contentious as the last one. Why is it so hard for her to turn her mother down? Will she ever learn to say no?

She plunges her hands into the cool water and smooths her wet palms over her face, massaging her eyelids. When she opens her eyes, Jeff's reflection floats behind hers in the window. She pulls a towel from the rack and blots her face dry.

"Can we talk?"

Liz drains the lettuce, puts it in the salad spinner, and dries her hands. "You first."

Watching him watch her in the reflection, she takes soup bowls and salad plates from the cupboard and turns to face him.

Elbows bent, thumbs tucked into his belt, he leans against the counter beside the stove, hands relaxed. As if about to deliver a prepared speech, he clears his throat. "After you wrecked my car, I realized I had wrecked our relationship, that I'd given you all the reasons you needed to break up with me." He forces a smile. "Seventeen years is long enough, don't you think? 'Time heals all wounds'?"

"Let bygones be bygones?" Wasn't that what her mother had said to her earlier? Liz concentrates on the pattern in the tile floor, black-on-white concentric boxes, like a maze closing in on her.

He scoffs. "Something like that, yes."

"Except in the moment right after it happened, crashing into your car didn't make things better. It didn't help me get over being mad— at you or Sunny. Maybe you guessed?" She looks at him.

"You're not sorry about the car?"

"Are you sorry about Sunny?"

He raises his eyebrows.

"Flirting with Sunny, remember?"

"Flirting." He says it the way you say an unfamiliar word to get comfortable with it, practicing the sound and feel of it. "That's what I told you. Only that's not exactly what happened."

"What *exactly* did happen?"

"Sunny wasn't an innocent bystander. Not innocent and not a bystander."

"I don't understand." Hadn't Jeff and Sunny admitted their behavior?

"I'll tell you." Sunny steps out of the shadowy hall into the bright kitchen, her eyes looking past Jeff, watching Liz. She closes the kitchen door behind her.

"Sunny." Jeff faces her, hands clenched by his sides.

Sunny keeps going, speaking to Liz as if Jeff weren't there. "I had a crush on Jeff. You teased me about it, remember? I was just your little sister, is what you thought. So I decided to go after him. Once I got him to drive me home, it was easy to get him to do other things. I was sorry about the car. But I wasn't sorry about the rest."

"The rest?" Whatever Sunny has to say, whatever she and Jeff had done, Liz has to know. Now. For two days after she rammed the Impala, Liz had locked herself in the guest room, leaving it only when she was certain no one was at home. Jeff had phoned. Each time her mother came to the door to appeal to her to talk to him, Liz had responded with silence. Once, her father had stood in the hallway, berating her for having caused "such a ruckus." Only Sunny had left her alone. Because she was embarrassed, Liz had thought then. Hadn't she flirted with Jeff in exchange for rides in his big blue car, his pride and joy?

"We had sex in the backseat every time he drove me home. I'm still amazed no one ever caught us."

Jeff shakes his head. Sunny, hands in her pockets, shoulders hunched, stares at the floor. Liz turns off the stove and ladles soup into the bowls. She wipes her hands and turns around, taking them both in in a glance. Out on the porch, Charles, Judith, and Jessie laugh. Above the sink, the clock ticks off the seconds. Across the kitchen from one another, Jeff and Sunny now stare at her, as if awaiting a verdict.

In that moment, in the aftermath of Sunny's admission, Liz sees the station wagon pull in front of the Impala, backing into it hard enough, fast enough, to knock off the front bumper. She hears the clang when it hits the ground. It is like standing at the train station, hearing the roar of the express train, feeling the throb of the platform as the train approaches and passes by, leaving her there, alone in the dark.

Liz picks up two bowls and motions to Jeff and Sunny to carry the others.

o o o

Several candles burn low, nearly down to the candlestick. Liz blows out the two nearest to her. The reflections of the others gleam in the wine glasses and in six pairs of eyes meeting and parting over the table.

"When we were little, on evenings like this, Sunny and I collected fireflies." Liz looks across the table, at Jeff, watching him settle back in his chair, his face expressionless. Sitting next to her, her mother chuckles.

"We'd poke air holes in the lid of an old jar, put some grass in the bottom, and catch as many as we could until we got bored. We shared a room then. We had twin beds. We put the jar on the nightstand between us, falling asleep as the pale glow faded. In the morning, Sunny took the jar out to the garden and emptied it." She clears her throat. "I always cried."

Across from Liz, Sunny looks down at the table.

"She always told me we'd catch more. 'Just wait 'til tonight, Lizzie.'" Liz looks around the table, her eyes lingering for a moment on Jeff, sitting across from her between Sunny and Jessie. "But the story always ended the same way: Catching more just meant having more dead fireflies the next morning."

Jeff slides his chair back, away from the table, and grips the top of Jessie's chair.

"Of course, we didn't know then what those flashing lights meant."

"What do you mean?" Jessie leans forward; Lizzie has fallen asleep.

"The males are show-offs," Liz says. "They're all looking for love. First come, first served."

"And the females?"

"They hang around, check out the goods," Liz shrugs. "But they don't flash until they spot The One. What a reversal, eh? It's the females who get to choose."

Across the back lawn, on the other side of the garden, a few fireflies flash erratically, their lights fading in the dark.

Sheba

Fall 2016

No more dogs, they decided, when Molly died.

Only a week ago, Emmy and Dan had sat on their living room floor, cradling Molly, talking to her, while the vet gave her the injection.

Emmy's knees and Dan's back made the case: Neither of them was physically up to taking on and keeping up with a puppy.

o o o

A year later, Emmy came home from school one afternoon to find Dan in the kitchen, peeling an onion, ingredients for meatloaf spread out on the counter, the radio tuned to the local jazz station.

She turned on the tap, filled a glass of water, and leaned against the breakfast bar. "Remember my student, Susie? That dairy farm up in the valley?"

Dan nodded. And smiled.

"They have a litter of puppies. Mom's a stray they took in. She's a mix. Chihuahua and Rat Terrier, they think."

"Small dog, then."

Emmy nodded. "Two females, two males, black and white. They're four months old." She reached across the counter to turn down the radio, giving him time.

"You up for a drive?"

"How about tomorrow after school? I should be home by 3."

Dan shook his head, grinning. "Four, four-month old puppies. Bet they're a handful."

"Rarin' to go," Emmy said.

Dan turned back to the meatloaf. What will be, will be.

o o o

They named her Sheba after Emmy's first dog.

"Sheba," they said in unison, looking down at her.

Sitting on the dark-red braided rug, ears pricked, head cocked, Sheba wagged her tail. Dan laughed and scooped her up. At four months, she weighed a bit over a pound and fit in the palm of his hand.

She was a burrower. A heat-seeking missile. "That's the Chihuahua in her," Emmy said. In the morning, as soon as she heard the furnace switch on, she headed straight for a floor vent, where she stretched out, turning over periodically, warming herself. Although it took Emmy and Dan some time to adjust to her size, to be careful not to step on her—Molly had been thirty times larger, Dan figured—Sheba learned fast, dodging their feet or finding places to watch and wait, out of their way.

When they watched TV, she slept curled up on the sofa between them, paws tucked under her chest.

Emmy traced the curve of the line between black and white that ran from behind Sheba's right ear, around her neck, down to her chest, over her left haunch to the right one. "Like yin and yang. Black meets white. Balance, duality, not opposition. The Chihuahua is our guardian; the Rat Terrier, our provider. It's almost a contract: We're here for her, she's here for us."

"Or maybe a Mallomar?"

"That marshmallow cookie?" Emmy giggled.

Sheba opened one eye and thumped her tail.

"Guess who likes that one?" Dan squeezed Emmy's shoulder.

o o o

The phone rings. Pencil in hand, drawing spread out on his drafting table, Dan picks up.

"This is Sergeant Scott, Mr. Olson. Connecticut State Police. There's been an auto accident at the Ardmore intersection. Your wife was injured; they're taking her to the ER now."

It's 7:30. Emmy had left with Sheba at 7:00. A quick trip to the Post Office, she'd said. He hears sirens and voices in the background. The hiss of rain. "Who else was involved?"

"We'll answer your questions at the hospital, sir."

Dan gets into the car. Adjusts the rearview mirror. Turns on the wipers. Across the road from their house, beyond the guardrail, the underbrush and trees loom in the mist. Leaves drift down, piling up along the road. He'd have to rake tomorrow. Tomorrow? As if it would be a normal Saturday, a Saturday of gardening, grocery shopping, laundry. He flicks his hi-beams once, checking for deer.

It must be bad. Otherwise, wouldn't Emmy have called him herself? In the dark fog beyond the headlights, as if projected on a movie screen, he sees Emmy's head, crushed against her car's windshield; Emmy lying on the pavement, the drizzle thinning her blood to a pale pink stream streaked with gasoline, mud. And Sheba? What about Sheba? Calm down. He hears Emmy's voice, as if she were in the car with him.

They joked sometimes about turning back the clock, made a game of it. "If only we'd bought that ski condo fifteen years ago. Bet it's worth a bundle now. We could sell it and retire to St. John's." If only. If only Emmy had waited until tomorrow to make her run to the Post Office. Irritated, Dan thinks, what was so urgent it had to get there tonight? It was too late to make Friday's outgoing mail pick-up and Saturday's mail isn't picked up until 5:00 p.m.

Pay attention, Dan, he hears Emmy say. Slow down.

At the traffic light, a four-way intersection at the entrance to the shopping center, flashing blue lights shine through the misty drizzle, now blowing in curtains across road. Traffic on both sides slows to a crawl as the right lane merges with the left. Dan peers into the murk, looking for Emmy's car. In his Jeep, he can see over and around the other vehicles. He flips on the directional signal to pull over to the shoulder. In the middle of the road, a trooper holds up both hands, palms out. Dan stops. Still no sign of Emmy's car.

Police cars line both sides of the road; a fire engine has parked on the diagonal across the intersection. Silhouetted figures cross back and forth, some bent over as if examining the pavement, others upright, conferring in pairs.

The trooper waves his flashlight again. Dan moves on past the entrance to the shopping center, past the sign, "Ardmore Hospital, 3 miles." Just beyond the sign, under the traffic light, across the intersection, Emmy's Volvo station wagon straddles the left lane, the front passenger door crumpled. It's too dark to see any other damage. *The windshield*, Dan thinks. *What about the windshield?* A tow truck pulls out in front of Dan hauling the pick-up. Shattered glass lies strewn across the road.

o o o

"Mr. Olson?" Outside the ER entrance, the state trooper waves him over. "Please come this way, sir."

A half-dozen adults, two of them holding small children on their laps, wait their turn in the registration area. Staring at the wall behind the desk, a woman in a mink coat holds an ice pack over her right eye. The man next to her hangs his head. Old enough to be her husband, Dan thinks. Is he responsible?

Two receptionists sit behind the desk. Both dark haired, one of them wears a ponytail, the other a short, tousled style. A short shag,

Emmy explained the day she came home from the beauty parlor, her shoulder-length hair cut in the same style.

"Sir?" The trooper gestures for him to take a place in the line.

Dan and the trooper are about the same height. The trooper is bulkier, kitted out in hat, boots, and rain gear, eyes wide, face set.

"What happened?"

"A two-car collision. Your wife has a concussion and a broken collarbone. The trauma team is checking her out now."

"I want to see her." To his own ears, Dan's voice sounds hollow, like it's coming from far away.

"First you need to fill out a few forms. Someone will be out to talk to you shortly."

Dan looks across the waiting room to the swinging door a few steps beyond the registration desk. Concussion? Broken collarbone? What else? He moves to the left around the trooper, who grabs his arm. Dan shakes him off. The trooper steps in front of him, legs spread wide, a wrestler's stance, arms by his sides.

"Mr. Olson, if you'll just step over here to the desk," he nods at the receptionists, who stare at them, wide-eyed. "It won't take long, sir."

It's like a dream he'd had. He knew where he was and where he was going, but the harder he tried, the more lost he became. People come and go; the PA blares gibberish.

Do what the guy says, Dan. Emmy again.

In college, he had taken Emmy to a Bob Dylan concert. The concert had sold out. Somehow, he and Emmy had got separated as they approached the head of the line. When he tried to cross over to join her, a guy had blocked his way. "Get back in line, you."

Dan shoved him; the guy shoved back. "Cut that out!" Emmy— five foot four, ninety-five pounds—stood between them. "Get over yourselves." She had taken Dan's arm and pulled him back in line. When he had tried to talk to her about it later, she'd put her hand on his arm and said, "Sometimes? Just do what the guy says."

The receptionist asks him about Emmy, questions he can answer by rote. Medications? Alcohol or drug use? Chronic conditions? Family doctor?

"Two. Dr. Jones is her internist. The other one, I can't remember her name. Give me a moment." The nurse looks up at him. She has glittery green eyes. Contacts? Dan opens his wallet. There's Emmy, cross-legged on the floor, smiling up at him, holding Sheba in her lap the day they picked her up. He had trimmed the photo to fit the plastic window.

He turns to the trooper. "Where's Sheba?"

"Sheba?" The trooper looks at the nurse, who shrugs.

"Our dog. She was with Emmy."

"There was no dog in the car, sir."

"I don't understand. She took the dog with her."

"Was she going to the shopping center?"

What difference does it make where Emmy was going? What does that have to do with Sheba? "Downtown," Dan tells him. "To the Post Office. She took the dog with her." Dan closes his eyes, visualizing Emmy's drive, past the woods between their house and the shopping center, through the light at the intersection, to the blinking light at the "Business District" sign a half-mile from the shopping center. She would have turned right and driven through the business district to the Post Office, depositing her package in the mailbox next to the entrance. Fifteen minutes, easy. Even in the rain. "She should have been home long ago."

The trooper searches Dan's face, takes him by the arm again, guides him to a chair and sits down with him. Leaning close, he speaks in a low voice.

"The other driver ran the light at the intersection and collided with your wife."

"Driver's side?" Dan asks.

"Passenger side."

"What about the other driver?"

"Sorry, sir." The trooper looks down at the floor, as though the answer to all this, the solution to this problem, lies there. "We've got our investigators there now, examining the vehicles, talking to witnesses."

Another trooper approaches with a black plastic bag, like a trash bag, hands it to Dan, "Your wife's personal effects, sir."

In the bag, Dan finds Emmy's pocketbook, cell phone, and car keys. And Sheba's bed, the one they use in the car. There's also a package, a prepaid Priority padded envelope. What was so important that Emmy had to make a trip to the Post Office in the rain, in the dark? Dan turns it over. It's addressed to Emmy's mother—her birthday present.

Dan hefts the package, nearly weightless. Dan, please. You know how she is about her birthday, Emmy's voice says.

o o o

The trooper holds out his card. "We'll make sure you get a copy of the accident report, Mr. Olson. The medical staff will take it from here." He nods toward the nurses. "She's in good hands, you know." He smiles. "I'll tell the fellows on the scene about your dog. The name is Sally, you say?"

"Sheba. Like the Queen of Sheba." Too much info, Dan, Emmy says. "Female. Black and white. Six pounds." The trooper writes it down.

A nurse appears. In her fifties, probably, her hair salt-and-pepper gray, she wears a breast-cancer ribbon pinned to the collar of her uniform, no makeup, no lipstick, and rimless glasses fastened to one of those lanyard things. "You may come with me now, Mr. Olson." She smiles at Dan, a neutral, greeting-type smile.

"To see Emmy?"

"Soon, sir. She's still in surgery."

When they reach the other side of the swinging doors and enter the waiting room outside the OR, the nurse gestures at the sitting area. With its padded armchairs, upholstered couches, and reading lamps, it reminds Dan of a model home living room, staged to create an illusion of ease and comfort. "I'll check back here in a while," the nurse says. "If you need anything, just ask."

"How long, do you think?"

She shrugged. "That depends. But I'll let you know as soon as I can. For now, try to imagine your wife well, at home, doing what she likes to do. Good vibes help." She smiles and pats his shoulder.

o o o

He wakes dry-mouthed, slumped down in the armchair, disoriented and light-headed. It feels like jetlag. The magazine he'd been paging through lies on floor. He had been running hard in his dream. Toward or away from something? Someone?

The answer teases him. A woman, laughing. Emmy? The laugh pitching higher and higher until it's a scream. Emmy, in pain, afraid, running. Sheba there too, as if offstage, in the wings of a huge, dark theater, getting smaller and smaller. Something or someone chasing Emmy? Sheba running away? Where was Sheba?

A hand on his shoulder, gentle, firm pressure. "Mr. Olson? Would you like something to drink?" The grey-haired nurse holds out a cup of water. He squints up at her against the lights.

Dan yawns. "Sorry." Fluorescent lights. Buzzing. His head throbs. "What time is it?"

"Almost 2:00 a.m. It's Saturday morning. Emmy's in the recovery room. She came through just fine."

He had told Emmy once he had forgotten how to cry, hadn't cried since he broke his arm in the sixth grade. Now, he touches his face, wet with tears. He stands, then sits, shaking his head. "Woozy."

"Take a couple of slow, deep breaths," the nurse instructs him. "Just take it easy."

"How many miles to the snack machine?"

"Breathe," she says. "Down in the cafeteria. The elevator is at the end of the corridor. Not even a mile." She chuckles.

Eyes closed, Dan inhales and exhales, until he can stand at last, steadier this time. The nurse pats his shoulder. "One step at a time."

Its lights dimmed at this hour, lined with doors closed on darkened rooms, the corridor stretches in front of him, silent now except for the sound of his footsteps and the occasional crackle of the loudspeaker. From the window at the end of the corridor, he looks out on the parking lot, the streetlights shuddering in the wind. The rain has stopped. A white bag skitters across the pavement into the chain link fence.

Sheba.

He'd heard of pets lost or left behind, reunited months later with their humans. If Sheba had escaped from the wreckage uninjured, could she find her way home? It's only two miles from the shopping center to their house. What if someone found her? What if they put her in a cage, out in the cold, without food, without water, and punished her if she barked or whined?

Pull up your socks, Emmy says. Make a plan, Dan.

"Mr. Olson?"

The receptionist—how long had she been standing there?

"Dr. Hellerman will see you now."

o o o

When he gets back to the recovery waiting room, the nurse stands by his chair, holding a clipboard. "Dr. Hellerman will be out momentarily, Mr. Olson." When she grins, he notices her crooked eye-tooth. It lifts her right lip just enough to give her an almost impish air. He grins back. "Emmy's orthopedic surgeon," she tells him. "The one who fixed her collarbone, Miracle Mike, we call him."

The doors from the OR area open and the surgeon swings through, his coat flowing around him like a cape. Miracle Mike and Superman? Erect, awake, smiling, Hellerman is in his mid-forties, fit and happy to see Dan, it appears.

After shaking Dan's hand, he takes a seat, leans back, stretches out his legs, ankles crossed, and hooks his thumbs into his waistband, as if he and Dan were old friends, jawboning after golf.

"Your wife was unconscious when she came in earlier. We gave her a thorough work up to make sure she hadn't suffered a skull fracture or a brain injury. She's a lucky gal. Just a concussion." Hellerman smiles, sits up and leans forward toward Dan, readying him for the punchline.

"'Just a concussion'?" The back of Dan's neck prickles the way it does when he gets mad. Watch it, Emmy's voice says. This guy put me back together. Besides, concussions are probably a dime a dozen to him. Suck it up, honey.

"A mild one." Hellerman straightens his tie. "Also some lacerations and contusions. Our plastic surgeon came in and took care of the wound to her forehead." He clears his throat. "Over her left eye." He scrutinizes Dan, as if to be sure he's following. Satisfied, he goes on, "She also has a broken collarbone, Mr. Olson, a comminuted fracture."

"What is that?"

"That means her collarbone shattered, pushed, and twisted at the same time. I gathered the pieces, stuck them back together, and wired her up." He smiles, affirmative, reassuring.

Dan thinks of the softness between Emmy's collarbone and the base of her neck, the vulnerability of it, a place he has kissed with affection and passion. "What will happen to those wires?"

"After she heals—it will take a while, I'm afraid—we'll see."

"About what?"

"Whether to leave or remove them. Either way, she'll be fine. Good as new. Collarbones are fragile, considering what they do for us. Putting one like your wife's back together can be tricky. Of course, the fragments aren't labeled. It's like trying to reassemble a split log where you have matchsticks, toothpicks, and chips—even sawdust. If you don't get the pieces into place just so, well, at worst, there'll be an infection to clean up. Or the bone might heal crooked and weak."

He pauses from time to time, positioning each phrase as carefully as he had positioned the fragments of Emmy's collarbone. "Any other questions?"

"I want to see her." That's a demand, Dan, not a question, Emmy says. Remember, this guy is my doctor.

"As soon as we move her out of recovery. That won't be for several hours. I suggest you go home now. Eat something. Get some sleep."

Dan stands. "Now, please."

Hellerman sighs. "I'll send someone out. You'll be able to see your wife through the window. That will have to do, for now. She's going to be just fine, Mr. Olson." When he puts his right hand on Dan's shoulder, Dan notices the blood spots. Three drops, two of them smaller than the third, on the front of his scrubs.

o o o

Dan cups his hands and leans against the glass to peer in at Emmy, lying in a web of tubes and wires, pale as the sheets draped over her. The BP and heart-rate monitor—at least that's what Dan thinks it is—shows a regular pattern of streaming ups and downs. He can see her face in profile, right side. No sign of the wound to her forehead. Then he remembers: Left side. He blows her a kiss, imagines it landing on her cheek, presses his palm against the window.

At the registration desk, the receptionist smiles up at him. "Come back later, mid-morning, say. We have your number in case we need you."

"Need me for what?"

Her eyes slide away. "If there's any change."

"Like if she wakes up, you mean?"

"For instance, if she's in any distress, you know, if we have to call the doctor back in." She can't—or won't—look at him now.

"It's okay. Thanks." Dan can't think of anything else to say to this twenty-five-year-old who is trying so hard to be a grown-up.

When Emmy wakes she'll want to know about Sheba.

o o o

Fallen branches and ragged drifts of leaves clutter the shoulder of the road. When Dan reaches the shopping center, all that remains of the accident are skid marks and a couple of orange cones, abandoned in the gutter.

The shopping center is deserted at 4:30 a.m.; there's no traffic, no one to become impatient with him for slowing to peer into the brush beyond the shoulder. By the time he pulls into the driveway, he has a plan to find Sheba.

o o o

At eight o'clock, with the flyers he has made and Emmy's package in hand, Dan makes his first stop at the gravel road that forms a T-intersection with the main road halfway between home and the shopping center. There's a cluster of mailboxes next to a stop sign and a message board nailed to a post.

Dan gets out of the car with a box of thumbtacks and attaches a flyer to the message board. "Help! I'm lost!" He averts his eyes, swallows hard, and looks at the color photo. Emmy had taken it. Sheba sits on the Bokhara rug looking up at the camera, head cocked, eyes wide, ears pricked. Black muzzle, head, and ears, white chest and legs, black back, white-tipped tail. Her markings stand out against the rug's red and blue pattern.

Printed in bold 18-point type, the rest of the flyer reads:

"My name is Sheba. I was in a car accident at the shopping center on Friday. If you see or find me, call Dan, 545-6606." He had considered the pros and cons of adding "Reward" at the bottom of the page. In the end, he had decided against the idea because he feared he'd get crank calls. Weren't things bad enough?

A car pulls up the lane. The driver rolls down the window. "Hey, Dan." The man smiles a friendly how-you-doing smile, the kind of greeting you offer a neighbor first thing in the morning.

Dan's face feels frozen. "Hey, Jack."

"Everything all right?"

Dan knows he has to say something. "Everything is not all right"? Then he'd have to explain what had happened. Tell the story. He opens his mouth. Nothing. When he tries again, he finds himself high above the scene, looking down on the red smudge of his jacket, the mud, the dark gravel, detritus left by the storm.

He feels the sensation in his groin, then under his tongue, a sensation he associates with panic attacks he'd had in elementary school when he was called on and didn't know the answer. Dry-mouthed, he swallows hard, leaning against the Jeep, struggling to catch his breath. Jack scrambles out of his car.

Dan hands him a flyer.

"Jeez, Dan, Sheba? A car accident?"

Dan nodded, wiping away his tears. "Emmy's in the hospital. Broken collarbone. On my way there now."

Jack stares at him, mouth agape, looks at the flyer in his hand, shaking his head. "What can I do?"

Panic, again. This time Dan breathes deep and slow, thinking about Emmy, pale and still in the recovery room. "Thanks. I'll let you know. Gotta go."

He takes the flyer to the message boards at the Stop & Shop, the UPS store, and Sears, then drives into town to the Post Office. About to drop Emmy's package into the mailbox, he notices the heart around "Ann" and an exclamation point after "Dunham." Emmy's gesture makes him smile. Three thousand miles away in Santa Barbara, Ann will celebrate her birthday next Tuesday. Or maybe it's Wednesday? By that time, Emmy will be home.

Sheba, too, Emmy whispers in his ear.

Between the shopping center and the hospital, Dan makes three more stops to tack flyers on telephone poles at the 7-Eleven, the Shell station, and the Mr. Fix-it shop. Later, he'll put flyers up on the other side of the road.

Later. After he checks on Emmy.

o o o

A new receptionist —blond pageboy, in her 40s, dimpled smile—sits at the registration desk. 9:00 a.m. Fourteen hours since Emmy left the house with Sheba.

"Can I help you?" The nurse's voice, younger than her appearance, reminds him how much he likes Emmy's voice, which—to him—sounds like honey tastes, warm and sweet. He doesn't correct her. Emmy would have. The difference between "can" and "may" is one of the ten rules she posts on her bulletin board. She had cleaned up his act, too.

"Sir?"

He gives her his name. Again. Explains why he's here. Again. Like *Groundhog Day*. Get a grip, Dan. Be a grown-up, Emmy's voice says.

"How is Emmy?"

The nurse checks the computer. "She had a good night, it says here. She's resting comfortably."

"'Resting comfortably'?" The only way Emmy could have 'rested comfortably,' was in her own bed, next to him, with Sheba burrowed under her fleece blanket between them.

The nurse gives him a tight smile and squares her shoulders. "That means she had no aftereffects from the anesthetic, she doesn't have a fever, and her vitals are normal as apple pie." Her eyes dare him to question her.

"Thanks," Dan mutters.

The swinging door opens and the floor nurse he'd met last night appears. "Let's go say good morning to Emmy, shall we?"

In a private room, Emmy lies on her back, like Gulliver tied down by the Lilliputians. That much is the same. Earlier, he'd seen her in profile. Now, he examines her face. How well he knows its topography: the curve of her forehead where it folds into her hairline; her eyebrows, with their tipped-up outer edges, one, a bit higher than the other; her eyes, closed, so that the thick lashes cast a slight shadow; narrow bridge of her nose; the twin peaks of her upper lip, which parts in a narrow gap above the lower one's full curve; her dimpled chin. He catalogs every line, every freckle, every scar. The incision over her left eye.

"Two black eyes?"

The nurse puts her hand on his arm. "From when she hit her head. Just bruises, Mr. Olson."

He stares at Emmy's eyes, waiting for them to open.

"Why don't you sit in this chair? It's okay to hold her hand. It's good to do that, you know. She'll wake soon."

Dan takes Emmy's right hand between both of his. Warm and relaxed, it feels like a small animal, like Sheba when she was a puppy. Except that Sheba had sniffed and licked, nuzzling his fingers, curious to find out more.

"I'm here, Em," he whispers.

She opens her eyes. Like the princess in the fairy tale.

"Dan?" She tries to sit up.

"Easy does it, now. Let me help." He fumbles until he finds the right button. The mattress inclines a couple of inches, raising Emmy's upper body. In a sling strapped around her waist, Emmy's left arm is immobilized against her chest.

Dan strokes her right hand.

"Thirsty." Her voice is hoarse.

Dan holds a cup with a straw to her mouth. She takes a sip, licks her lips.

"Tell me."

As Dan tells her what he knows, in his mind's eye he recreates the accident like a scene in a movie: the two vehicles approaching the traffic light, the dark, rainy night. He watches the light change to green. The car with the right of way, Emmy's Volvo, continues into the intersection at a moderate speed. The other vehicle, a Ford pick-up, accelerates to run the red light, hits the passenger side of the Volvo, pushing it across the intersection onto the shoulder. Rescue workers find Emmy stretched across the Volvo's passenger seat, seatbelt fastened, torso twisted, left over right, her head wedged under the dashboard.

The 17-year-old driver of the truck dies instantly.

"Seatbelt?" Emmy asks.

"No seatbelt." Dan says, as if that explains everything

Emmy touches the incision in her forehead. "This?"

"The passenger window shattered."

"And this?" She gives her left arm a tentative pat.

"Fractured collarbone. Lots of pieces, all wired and put back to-gether, safe at home, thanks to Dr. Hellerman."

Emmy's eyes open wide. "Sheba?"

"She got out of the car somehow. That's all I know."

It's as if they're at opposite ends of a narrow bridge over a deep gorge. Emmy takes the first step. "I've been trying to remember what happened just before the crash." Because it was a short round trip—a half-hour at most—she had carried Sheba out of the house, put her into the dog bed on the passenger seat.

"She didn't have her coat. No harness. No seatbelt." Emmy sobs. "Who ran into me, Dan?"

"A senior. Kid by the name of Joe Sterne."

"Joe?" Her eyes widen. "He's one of my 'Step Up' kids, the boy I was telling you about the other day."

A high school English teacher for thirty years, Emmy had created the 'Step Up' program for kids with dyslexia. She had written the materials for it and trained teachers statewide to use it.

"He's doing so well, Dan. Like a sponge," she says now. "He works so hard. He even helps the others. What am I saying?" Her eyes widen in their bruised sockets. "I meant '*was* doing so well.' Joe, dead. Sheba , lost." She sobs. "No seatbelt." Gasping for breath, she tries to roll over, to get out of the bed. Dan holds her close and pushes the call button.

After the nurse adjusts the sedation IV and leaves, Dan takes Emmy's hand. "Here's what we know, Em. Sheba wasn't in the car when the rescue team found you." And wasn't lying in the road, or on the shoulder nearby when I drove past. He keeps this to himself. "She might be hurt. She might be hiding. That's why I'm going to look for her. No more catastrophizing."

Emmy squeezes his hand.

Dan kisses her forehead.

o o o

Back at the house, he makes a sandwich and some instant coffee and calls the insurance agent. There are phone messages. Emmy's best friend, Allison, also a teacher: "Call me, Dan." Jack's wife, Nan, who often hikes with Emmy: "I've made you a casserole, Dan. I'll leave it on the back porch. Call us if you need anything." Avery, his partner: "I just heard about Emmy. Sorry for the kid, for his parents especially. Maybe his hothead friends will get it: Obey the law, you idiots. Let me know what you need, partner. Love to Emmy."

He takes out his topographical map and begins plotting his search of the twenty-five-acre woodland lying between their house and the shopping center on the east side of the two-lane paved road. He'll tackle the other side of the road—about twelve acres of rocky outcrops, pine forest, and brush—tomorrow.

That afternoon, he takes a path that runs into the woods between their home and the shopping center, a path he has often followed on his birdwatching forays. Destined for a housing development, this is the last privately owned undeveloped piece of a forest that once stretched north and south along the river.

The tops of the oaks and the maples gleam orange, red, and gold in the afternoon sun. Now and again, flashes of white catch his eye. He stops. Looks through his binoculars into the woods: bits and piec-es of trash have drifted downhill from the road. Bird calls pierce the drone of afternoon traffic, echoing across the valley from the inter-state five miles away.

"Sheba! Here girl!"

Just off the track, Dan spots a rabbit skeleton, narrow skull pressed into the soil, ribs detached from the spine, rear leg bones separated at the joints. Nearby, a tuft of fur clings to a clump of grass, as if hiding.

If Sheba survived the accident, if she's injured and holed up somewhere, tonight will be her second night in the woods, where coyotes, foxes, and raccoons prowl. Sheba isn't much larger than the rabbit. Keep going, Dan, Emmy's voice urges. There's not much daylight left.

On his way back to the house at dusk, he hears the call of a red-tailed hawk wheeling high above him, preparing to dive and strike. Its eyesight sharp enough to see a mouse from 100 feet, it would have no trouble spotting Sheba, even at dusk. Holding his binoculars steady, Dan watches the woods around him, waiting for the flash—the white tip of Sheba's tail.

The hawk cuts away. For now, its prey—rabbit, mouse, squirrel, or Sheba—is safe.

o o o

The next morning, sitting up with a magazine in her lap, Emmy smiles. Her bruises seem darker. Dan closes his eyes. Opens them. Smiles back.

"I've been so good, they're going to keep me one more day," she announces.

Hugging his bouquet of flowers, Dan twirls around and bows, with a flourish: "At your service, Madame."

Emmy laughs.

"Shall I take this bouquet home?"

She mock-frowns and waves him over to the credenza, at an array of vases, including one of long-stemmed white roses.

"A secret admirer?"

"Joe's parents." She leans back against the pillow, eyes closed. She opens them, takes a deep breath. Her voice catches. "A loving family. Considerate people, Dan. They were so proud of how well he'd done. That he was going to college next year." Her eyes hold his. "Sheba?"

Dan shakes his head. "I spent yesterday afternoon in the woods downhill from the road. No sign of her. No response to the flyers I posted. As soon as I leave here, I'm going back out."

Emmy pats the bed. Dan sits beside her.

"I want to tell you what I remember."

It had been raining for about an hour when she pulled out of the driveway. Since they hadn't had rain for a while, Emmy knew the paved road would be slick, so she took her time.

As she approached the traffic light at the Ardmore intersection it turned green. "I was going about 25, I think."

Dan nods. That's what was in the accident report.

"I don't remember seeing the truck. But I must have sensed it, because I let go of the steering wheel and threw myself over Sheba." Emmy stares across the room.

"That explains it."

"What?"

"You were across the passenger seat, down in the well, under the crushed passenger door. That's what caused the fracture and concussion." Dan gently traces the patch over the incision in her forehead.

Emmy leans her head back, eyes closed. "I can see her, just the way she was in her bed beside me in the car. Curled up, enjoying the ride the way she does." She opens her eyes.

Dan kisses her forehead, smooths her hair. "You think about coming home tomorrow." He stands and heads toward the door. He stops and turns toward her. "That package? I mailed it to your mother yesterday." Saturday morning. Seemed like a week ago. "Isn't her birthday Wednesday?"

"Tomorrow. I'll call her." She pats the sling and grimaces. "One more thing."

Dan waits. Emmy lifts her right arm and lets it drop, as if the weight is too much for her.

"Sheba huddled under my arm, her head tucked under my chin. That's the last thing I remember."

o o o

Back at the house for coffee and a sandwich, Dan picks up two phone messages: the pharmacy about the prescriptions ordered by Hellerman, and Dave, their mechanic. He listens to Dave's twice. "Gotta hand it to Volvo. The car saved Emmy's life. That's the good news, for sure." He sighs. "I can sell the vehicle for parts, Dan. I'll let you know in a few days. Call me after you talk to your insurance guy." Someone in the background speaks to Dave. "One more thing. We found a little pink pig, a squeaky toy, under the seat."

They keep Sheba's basket of toys next to the fireplace in the living room. First thing in the morning, after her breakfast, she begins her daily game: the removal of toys, one at a time, each one sniffed at or batted around. Dan picks up the blue, plush octopus, holds it to his nose, inhaling its faintly salty odor. Sheba.

Shopping together one day, he and Emmy had found the pink pig at K-Mart. At first, Sheba nuzzled and mouthed it, before picking it up and carrying it with her to her bed, where she licked it, head to toe and back again. Emmy gave it a squeeze. It squeaked. Sheba whined and pawed her. "I get it, sweetheart," Emmy patted her. "No more squeaking." Every night, Sheba carried the little pig to their bed and slept with it tucked under her chin.

Dave's discovery of the toy raises Dan's spirits. Grasping at straws? Emmy's voice again. "Any port in a storm," Dan says aloud, startling himself into a laugh.

o o o

Mid-afternoon, he drives up to the intersection and parks on the shoulder opposite the shopping center.

What Emmy had told him didn't help explain what might have happened to Sheba after the accident. Had she been injured? Had she escaped? Overhead, a squirrel leaps from branch to branch, harried by a couple of scolding crows. Focus, Emmy tells him.

This side of the road, the uphill side, is a jungle of blackberries and wild roses. On both sides of the narrow path, intertwining stems, some as thick as his wrist and covered in thorns, form an impenetrable barrier. Unless you're a rabbit, a chipmunk, or a six-pound dog. Here and there, Dan spots tufts of fur, grey for the most part. Although Sheba's short white hairs cling to their blankets, rugs, and fleece jackets, and even if she had run for cover, it's not likely there will be any trace of her hair out here.

Every few yards, he calls her. Only his echo responds.

At home again on the back porch, he removes his muddy pants and boots. As he rinses his boots, he hears the hawk cry. He scans the sky above the woods through the binoculars. Maybe it's hunting down by the river.

As agreed, he checks in with Emmy at the hospital, hearing in her voice the echo of the strain in his own.

"Anything?"

"I'll try again tomorrow."

"I'll be home tomorrow," Emmy says.

o o o

"Oh, my!"

His arm around her, Dan tries to see the scene through Emmy's eyes. Potted plants and bouquets occupy tables and shelves in the hallway, the living room, the kitchen. African violets and hyacinths, mixed bouquets, lilies, and roses perfume the air; their colors and textures catch the sunlight, brightening every corner.

Emmy leans her head against him. "So I'm not dreaming. This is home. I'm back."

Dan nods toward the bedroom. "Bed for you. Clean sheets and everything." She frowns up at him. "Doctor's orders, remember?"

"Lunch?"

"Your wish is my command, madame. The homecoming special will be ready momentarily."

At 2:00 p.m., Dan checks on Emmy, propped up on the pillows he arranged to support her back and shoulder.

"Monday. Three nights out there. Nearly four days." Emmy gazes out the window at the maple, its foliage a curtain of gold in the afternoon light. "I wish I could come with you."

"Visualize Sheba, think about all the things we love about her, imagine her safe, at home again with us." He heard the nurse, telling him nearly the same thing the night of the accident. He could no longer remember if he had tried to visualize Emmy well at home again. He remembered the feeling he'd had after the nightmare, when he woke. That sense of dread lay in his stomach now, like a pool of stagnant, cold water.

The corners of Emmy's mouth lift. Not quite a smile, but good enough for now.

o o o

He parks at the scene of the accident. The orange cones are gone; only the skid marks remain. The ruts left by the Volvo have dried out. A raccoon's paw prints cross them and disappear into the woods.

The sound and downdraft of powerful wings passing overhead startle him. The red-tailed hawk—the same one he had seen twice before—a rabbit limp in its talons. He hasn't yet told Emmy about the hawk.

On his first pass Sunday afternoon, Dan had spotted a second deer track parallel to the one he had taken. He zips his jacket, settles his cap and follows it now, ducking under the low branches and sinking ankle deep in the mud.

Thanks to walks they've taken in the woods below their house, Sheba knows that area. Dan thinks she'd have found her way home, had she crossed the road in that direction.

But what if she had run from the accident into the woods on this side of the road instead? Twenty yards in, the track dead-ends in a mass of multiflora, an invasive rose planted years ago to keep livestock from straying. If Sheba made her way up here and into it, she'd be safe from the hawk, at least. Grasping at straws again. What will he tell Emmy?

"Sheba!" The echo sounds once, as if switched off.

o o o

Emmy is awake, reading. She closes the book. "I had my 'happy birth-day' call with Mom. She was on her way to lunch with friends. I gave her the bare bones version." She folds and smooths the top sheet across her lap and adjusts the sling. "Dogs have a phenomenal hom-ing instinct, she said."

Dan holds her close. He reaches into his pocket. "Dave found this under the front seat."

Emmy's eyes fill. She takes it from him, rubs its tummy, holds it to her nose. "Two out of three."

"Two out of three?"

"The pig and me, two of us, home again."

"And Sheba makes three?"

Emmy sniffles and looks up at him. "I'm going to trust Sheba's homing instinct. Let's see what tomorrow brings."

o o o

For the first time in thirty years, they sleep apart. At Emmy's insis-tence. "At least one of us will get a good night's sleep."

On the pull-out couch in his office, Dan tosses and turns, until at last, sometime in the middle of the night, he falls deeply asleep. In his dream, he sees Sheba at the edge of a dark overgrown forest. When he calls, she turns and runs from him. No matter how fast he runs after her, she runs faster, until she's swallowed in the gloom.

Startled awake, Dan sits up. He hears a yip, faint but clear. On his way to the kitchen, he looks in on Emmy, sleeping propped up on sev-eral pillows. The nightlight in the corner of the room casts an amber glow against the wall. She murmurs, then sighs.

Another yip, then a thump. Dan picks up a flashlight and pads across the kitchen to the back porch. The garden is dark, the maples along the road sentries guarding the perimeter. He turns the knob quietly and opens the door.

Sitting on the porch, Sheba looks up at him through the screen door.

The kitchen light comes on. Emmy. "Sheba?"

Sheba creeps into the kitchen, ears low and flat against her head. She rolls over, belly up, her tail barely fluttering from side to side.

"She's apologizing. Oh, Dan." Holding his arm, Emmy lowers herself to sit on the floor. She strokes Sheba's head, "Good girl, such a good girl." Sheba cringes and yelps once. "What's this? On the back of her neck."

Dan kneels. Gingerly, he touches the spot. "A bite maybe? Two wounds, I'd say." Sheba trembles, whining deep in her throat. She's covered in dried mud. There are burs or thorns wedged between her toes. Dan brushes off the mud to take a closer look. "Two patches, more like deep scratches than a bite. I'll take her to the vet in the morning. I'm going to work on her feet now."

Dan helps Emmy stand and supports her as she sits on one of the kitchen chairs. He puts Sheba in her lap. "Can you steady her a bit?" Emmy turns slightly in the chair so that Sheba can settle into the curve of her right arm, facing Dan.

Gently using his fingertips, Dan clears the burs and thorns from between Sheba's toes. Once, she licks Emmy's hand. When Dan finishes, she stands and stretches, head and tail up, and jumps to the floor. She eats, then drinks, thirstily. Dan leaves the kitchen. When he returns, he squats beside Emmy and places the pink pig on the floor. Sheba picks it up, gives it a shake, lies down with it between Dan and Emmy.

"Three for three," Emmy says.

Acknowledgements

It takes a team to make a book. The writer selects the pieces and chooses how to arrange them and tell the story. But without the contributions of readers, editors, printers, friends, and family, it would never become a book. I am delighted at last to acknowledge my team of readers, editors, and advocates: John Hough, Joyce Krieg, Patricia Hamilton, John Powers, Mildene Bradley, Kristin Swanson, Sylvie Reynolds, Central Coast Writers, David Hermitte and Steve Henrikson.